# TRIV IN PURSUIT

As the classroom door swung open, Watling vaulted off Triv and back into his place. He was just in time. For no sooner had he crash-landed on to his chair than he was on his feet again as the whole class stood to attention, and into the room stormed the dreaded Kong.

Kong, the Headmaster of St Ethelred's.

Kong, whose real name was King.

Kong, who with his spiky, cropped hair, enormous build and arms which nearly reached his knees, bore a striking resemblance to the famous film gorilla.

The *dreaded* Kong, because he only ever counted in hun*dreds*.

"Two hundred lines, Trevellyan!" bellowed Kong.

Triv looked up from the floor, a pair of Watling-sized shoeprints stamped across the back of his blazer. He shut his eyes and waited for the rest.

"Two hundred times," bawled Kong. "'When the Headmaster enters the room, I show respect by standing up, not by lying down.' On my desk first thing Monday morning!"

# Michael Coleman

# TRIV IN PURSUIT

**RED FOX**

A Red Fox Book

Published by Random House Children's Books
20 Vauxhall Bridge Road, London SW1V 2SA

A division of Random House UK Ltd

London Melbourne Sydney Auckland
Johannesburg and agencies throughout the world

First published by The Bodley Head 1992

Red Fox edition 1993

Text © Michael Coleman 1992

Printed and bound in Great Britain by
Cox & Wyman Ltd, Reading, Berkshire

RANDOM HOUSE UK Limited Reg. No. 954009

ISBN 0 09 991660 6

*To TRIVs everywhere*

# Contents

# 1
# Now you see them . . .

Mr Stitson was the first teacher to disappear.

It happened on a Monday; by all accounts a fairly typical Monday for the roly-poly metalwork master.

He had spent the period before morning break preparing materials for the day ahead, thumping a variety of metallic strips into the shapes he wanted just so that classes like 3B could thump them back into shapes he didn't want.

Then after a trip to the staff room to pick up his regular mug of strong sweet tea, Mr Stitson had headed out for playground duty.

Two detentions later – dished out with some strong words about the perils of nicotine to a couple of first years he found smoking behind the science block – and Mr Stitson was back in the metalwork room showing 3B how to make an ashtray.

That Triv should be the last person to see Mr Stitson before the teacher went missing was pure chance.

Triv had had an equally typical Monday morning. Metalwork had been a disaster – again – and he had stayed behind to try and make his ashtray look more like an ashtray and less like a small bucket with dents in the side.

But within five minutes Stitson had emerged

from his tiny storeroom. He was still wearing the brown overall that everybody at St Ethelred's reckoned the nurse had wrapped him in at birth.

"Buzz off, Trevellyan," he'd said. "I need to get some lunch inside me before the bell goes and I have to face you lot again."

Triv had buzzed, but not before Stitson had passed judgement on his ashtray, now looking like a saucer that had been run over by a bus.

"Hopeless, Trevellyan!"

They were Mr Stitson's last recorded words.

When 3B came back after lunch the metalwork maestro was nowhere to be seen. He was not behind his bench; not in his storeroom; not in St Ethelred's at all. Nowhere.

All that remained was a note, attached to his workbench with a bent nail.

The handwriting was awful, the sort of slanting scrawl that Triv would never have been allowed to get away with.

Stitson's handwriting.

"Steel yourself," read the metalwork master's note, "I'm off."

\* \* \*

It was at about the same time next day, Tuesday, that Miss Derbyshire went to lunch and didn't come back.

Miss Derbyshire was St Ethelred's resident crackpot. A chilly mortal, Miss Derbyshire's outfit always included a fur coat, a fur hat and a pair of knee-length boots.

In class she would take off her hat and in summer, when the weather turned for the better, she would switch to ankle-length boots.

2

The fur coat was never, ever, removed.

Winter and summer, Miss Derbyshire sat huddled beside an oil-filled radiator and taught art.

Triv was about as bad at art as he was at metalwork; if anything, slightly worse.

For their current exercise they were supposed to be painting a landscape from an imaginative perspective. Triv had entitled his piece, "View From A Flagpole".

Miss Derbyshire had examined this masterpiece the previous week, summoning Triv into the warm glow of her presence.

"My dear boy," she had trilled, "this is an absolutely *perfect . . .*"

Miss Derbyshire had paused, searching for the right word. Then she'd found it. ". . . mess."

That's how it was that Triv came to be the first to learn that Miss Derbyshire had vanished as well.

Just for once, he had decided, he was going to produce a landscape with trees which looked more like trees and less like skeletons draped in some strange green lurgy. So, with the aim of getting his first few grotty attempts over and done with before Miss Derbyshire even turned up, Triv had nipped up to the art room early.

He'd found an empty room. Empty of Miss Derbyshire, that is. But not completely empty.

For there, squatting on the radiator like some furry creature sleeping off a heavy meal, he had discovered Miss Derbyshire's hat.

And the note.

It had been tacked to Miss Derbyshire's personal easel and was written in artistic copperplate lettering.

"Gone away," it read. "Get the picture?"

3

\* \* \*

Mr McDougall vanished on Wednesday.

At the first hint of rain Triv had shuffled quietly away from his goalkeeping duties in the playground Match of the Day and headed for the warm and musty geography room. He had half-expected Mr McDougall to be there already, pinning maps in readiness for 3B's lesson straight after lunch.

But the geography master was nowhere to be seen.

Only the note he'd left behind . . .

\* \* \*

It was Mr McDougall who had given Triv his nickname, some months before.

He had been talking . . . and talking . . . and talking . . . about the various bits that constitute the British Isles. Especially the bit he came from – Scotland.

"The Highlands . . . are ye listening? . . . the Highlands of Scotland occupy twenty-six thousand . . . listen . . . one hundred and thirty-six square kilometres. That is *twenty* . . . I say *twenty* times the size of that wee place called London."

As he spoke, Mr McDougall paced back and forth. He was a short man, shorter than most of the third year boys. Shorter even than some of the second year girls.

Triv, or plain James Trevellyan as he was then, had put his hand up.

"Please, sir, is that Greater London you mean, or the City of London?"

Mr McDougall had frowned. "What're ye on aboot, boy?"

4

"Because if it's Greater London, well, Greater London's area is one thousand five hundred and eighty square kilometres. That makes The Highlands sixteen-and-a-half times bigger, not twenty . . ."

The Geography teacher had glowered.

"Forget London then," he said, "the Scottish Highlands are *three* times the size of Yorkshire."

Triv put up his hand again. He liked facts. Metalwork and art required practical talents that he didn't have. But geography was about facts, and facts stuck to him like chewing gum to a desk. If facts were footballs, he'd have been goalkeeper for England by now.

"Is that just North Yorkshire, sir? Because if it's West Yorkshire and South Yorkshire as well as North Yorkshire, then the Highlands are only two-and-a-quarter times as big as . . ."

"The point I am trying te make, Trevellyan, is that the Scottish Highlands are not just big. They're *very* big!"

"Not compared to Texas, sir. Texas is ninety-two thousand four hundred . . ."

That was when it happened.

That was when Mr McDougall had drawn himself up to his full height and sent his broadest r-rolling accent echoing throughout the length and breadth of St Ethelred's.

"Trrrrriv-ial, Trrrrrevellyan! Ye hear me? I'm talking aboot Geography, not a game of Trrrrrivial Purrrrsooot!"

\* \* \*

And now Mr McDougall had disappeared as well, leaving just a note.

5

A note, pinned to a map of Scotland.

"I'm awa the noo," it read. "I've Dundee best I can."

* * *

The pattern changed on Thursday. Two teachers disappeared, not one.

Again, both left messages that were found at lunch time.

In one way, however, the disappearance of old Mr Winkler, the doddery music master, was different to the others. He didn't vanish at lunchtime. In fact, he hadn't turned up at St Ethelred's at all that day. It was just that nobody noticed until lunchtime.

Triv was a regular visitor to the music room. Not that he could play an instrument, he couldn't. He'd tried to learn the violin once but had given it up after the neighbours had reported him to the RSPCA on suspicion of cruelty to a cat.

No, Triv couldn't play an instrument. But Susan Frost could. Susan played the piano.

Susan, with her long blonde hair, was the girl of Triv's dreams. He would imagine them together on a summer's day, sitting in the cool shade of the oak tree at the far corner of the sports field, thumbing happily through the latest edition of the *Guinness Book of Records*.

One day, perhaps that might happen, when he could pluck up enough courage to ask her out. For now though, Triv's tactics were less ambitious.

They consisted of wandering up to the music room and standing outside the door. He'd listen to Susan Frost practise her scales on St Ethelred's ancient grand piano. And then, when she moved on to something more spectacular, like Beethoven or Lennon and McCartney, he'd wander in as though he'd nothing else to do and offer to turn the pages of her music.

On this Thursday, however, there were no tinkling scales when Triv arrived. Susan was not playing. She was standing outside the locked music room door, rattling helplessly at the handle.

She stopped when Triv pointed out the note.

It was taped to the door, underneath an advertisement about the forthcoming Music Festival. Mr Tinkler's message had been pencilled neatly along the staves of a sheet of manuscript paper.

"Gone away," it said. "And I won't be coming Bach."

\* \* \*

Then, first period that afternoon, 3B had what was probably their most successful ever period of conversational French.

Mademoiselle Balmain, petite and Parisienne, didn't come back from her dejeuner. She left a note, of course.

Triv didn't discover that one though. By the time he and Susan Frost had made their way past the metalwork room where class 2B were making darts in the absence of Mr Stitson, past the art room where 3A were painting dartboards ready for using 2B's darts, and past the empty geography room (5B having decided that Mr MacDougall would have wanted them to practise drawing contour maps of the skateboard park), somebody else had discovered it.

The honour went to Ingo English.

"Elle n'est pas ici," Ingo said accurately, even if his accent left a lot to be desired.

"Non, elle has hopped it," said his friend Watling, whose vocabulary was rather more limited.

And yet even Watling could understand the message which was chalked on the board in Mademoiselle Balmain's distinctive left-to-right lettering.

"Au revoir," was all it said.

"Elle a disparu," said Triv from behind them. "Et si vous me demandez, je pense qu'il a quelque chose poisson ici."

"You what?" said Ingo, turning round to see Triv looking at the board.

"Yeah, what you on about Trevellyan?" said Watling.

Triv smiled. He was good at French. But then he had a superglue memory. Unlike Ingo, whose memory was simply normal. And certainly unlike Watling, who often had trouble remembering how to spell "Watling".

"She's disappeared," Triv translated. "And if you ask me, I think there's something fishy going on here."

\* \* \*

Friday was a terrible day. Nobody vanished at all.

In fact, as far as 3B were concerned, quite the opposite happened.

Somebody turned up unexpectedly.

Somebody whose ability for causing terrible days to occur led them all to decide that the mystery of the missing teachers had to be solved without delay.

Somebody called Kong.

# 2
# Kong of the jungle

"Sssssssssssssshhhh! Kong's coming!"

Watling had been standing guard at the classroom door, his big square head stuck out into the corridor as though somebody was feeding him buns.

Now, still "Ssssshhh"-ing dramatically, the thicko of class 3B went to dive back to his place.

He didn't get very far. One of his size 9 feet turned to hurtle down the centre aisle. But the other, as if his brain had been unable to handle the problem of beaming signals down to both feet at once, stayed where it was.

As the moving foot hit the foot that wasn't moving, Watling began to fall. Desperately, he tried to save himself. Flailing wildly, he threw out a hand and grabbed hold of the first thing his fingers touched.

Had someone told him that a lumbering great Watling was going to seize hold of his tie, Triv might have been able to take evasive action. But they didn't, so he couldn't.

So one moment he was sitting quietly, wondering why podgy Mr Stitson, nutty Miss Derbyshire, pocket-sized Mr McDougall, antique Mr Winkler and la jeune Mademoiselle Balmain had left St Ethelred's in such mysterious circumstances. The next he was on the floor, this time wondering why

9

Watling seemed to have mistaken him for the north face of Mount Everest.

As the classroom door swung open, Watling vaulted off Triv and back into his place. He was just in time. For no sooner had he crash-landed on to his chair than he was on his feet again as the whole class stood to attention, and into the room stormed the dreaded Kong.

Kong, the Headmaster of St Ethelred's.

Kong, whose real name was King.

Kong, who with his spiky, cropped hair, enormous build and arms which nearly reached his knees, bore a striking resemblance to the famous film gorilla.

The *dreaded* Kong, because he only ever counted in hun*dreds*.

"Two hundred lines, Trevellyan!" bellowed Kong.

Triv looked up from the floor, a pair of Watling-sized shoeprints stamped across the back of his blazer. He shut his eyes and waited for the rest.

"Two hundred times," bawled Kong. " 'When the Headmaster enters the room, I show respect by standing up, not by lying down.' On my desk first thing Monday morning!"

"Yes, sir," said Triv, nodding slowly. He was calculating the full extent of the penalty.

"When the Headmaster," etc. etc. Twenty-one words, a short line for Kong. At three words per second, Triv's top writing speed if the words were to be readable, that came to seven seconds per line. One thousand four hundred seconds for two hundred lines. Twenty-three point three, three recurring minutes.

Could have been a lot worse, thought Triv. He

10

eased himself painfully back on to his chair, thankful that Watling hadn't been wearing football boots.

With a heavy, solemn, tread – like an undertaker with a busy day ahead of him – Kong strode to the centre of the classroom. He waited, his small eyes darting left and right, until it was so quiet you could have heard a pen drop.

Which it did. Triv's pen. Dislodged from his pocket in the scrum with Watling, it now clattered to the floor as he tried to straighten his tie.

" 'I will, at all times and in all places,' " intoned Kong instantly, " 'ascertain that my writing instruments, materials and all other items of scholarly paraphernalia, are firmly lodged about my person so as to remain *in situ* unless and until required, in order that at no time, by virtue of their unscheduled and unanticipated appearance, will they disturb the tranquillity of school life by descending to the floor.' "

Triv sat, open-mouthed.

"Two hundred . . ." began Kong. "No, let us make it a nice round number, shall we Trevellyan? . . . five hundred times, if you please."

Triv didn't bother to work it out. It was a lot.

Kong turned away from Triv and glared at the class in general.

"3B," he growled, "due to circumstances beyond my control a change is necessarily necessary in those arrangements normally appertaining to the matter of your tutelage . . ."

"What's he on about?" whispered Ingo English in Triv's ear.

Triv pretended he hadn't heard.

11

"Staff shortages of a temporary nature," Kong continued, "leave me with no alternative but to allocate my personal self as the sole instructional operative for this cohort of St Ethelred's pupils."

Kong paused, taking 3B's open-mouthed silence as a clear sign that they appreciated the importance of his statement. What it really meant was that they were all trying to work out what he was actually saying.

"You mean . . ." Ingo hissed a few seconds later.

Triv, who knew precisely what Kong was on about, nodded grimly. And silently.

"You mean he's . . ."

Triv nodded again.

Ingo persisted. "You mean . . . he means . . . he . . ."

Triv glanced up as Kong turned to write something on the blackboard.

"You mean . . . he . . ." Ingo's hiss had more than a hint of panic about it now. "Kong . . . Kong's taking us?"

Triv nodded once more. He looked up. Kong was now writing on the board. At last it was safe to speak.

"Yes," whispered Triv.

"Five hundred lines, Trevellyan!" bawled Kong. " 'I will resist the temptation to communicate verbally with my neighbour . . .' "

*　*　*

The day didn't get any better.

Metalwork with Kong saw Triv pick up another two hundred lines, even though he hadn't meant his ashtray to land on Kong's foot.

Ingo English had shown no sympathy at all.

12

"Dropped a bit of a clanger there, didn't we?" he smirked.

Art with Kong got him another hundred lines for saying, "Don't you mean Picasso, sir?" and interrupting Kong's story about the famous artist called Pickaxeo who used to smash up his paintings when they wouldn't go right.

But the worst was yet to come. The last period of the day was music with Kong.

Triv was determined to keep his head down and to say nothing.

He kept quiet during Kong's explanation that pop music was so called because it made your ears pop.

He said nothing when Kong talked about his favourite wind instruments, the clarinet, and the blowboe.

He even managed not to laugh, and not to cry, when Kong had joined Susan Frost in practising the piano duet that she and old Mr Winkler were due to play at the Music Festival.

And then, just as the lesson drew to a close, it all went wrong.

"Before you depart on your departure," growled Kong, "are there any questions?"

Silence. Triv bit his tongue. It was like having a lion ask you if you had anything he could eat.

Then, unbelievably, a hand went up. A milky-white hand, with long smooth fingers. A grade eight pianist's hand.

"Please, Mr King," said Susan Frost.

Triv's heart beat a little faster at the sound of that voice. So did Ingo's.

"Cor!" he breathed, giving Triv a nudge in the

ribs at the same time. "Our Susie's a nice bit of crackling."

Triv was on the point of saying something nasty to the uncouth Ingo when he caught sight of Kong's face. Kong, the dreaded Kong, the Kong whose features made one think that what they really needed to make them complete was a banana stuck in their midst . . . that very same Kong was actually smiling.

"Yes, Susan," he cooed, "what is it?"

"Are they coming back, sir? Mr Winkler and the others?"

Kong winced, as though somebody had jabbed him with a pin.

"That foreknowledge is not in my possession," he said, managing to maintain his composure.

"He doesn't know," hissed Ingo. He was beginning to get the hang of interpreting Kong's statements.

"Oh," said Susan. "I see."

"So until they return," beamed Kong, "I, your headmaster, will be your mentor."

It must have been the example of Susan's bravery that made Triv do it. Afterwards, as he sat writing out the lines it cost him, that was the only explanation he could come up with.

"Where have they gone, sir?" he called out.

"Yeah, what's going on?" cried Ingo, seizing what he saw as a great chance to impress the scrumptious Susie.

Even Watling joined in with a shout of "Yeah!" before asking the boy sitting next to him what they were talking about.

Kong's smile vanished. He pursed his lips. His

14

cheeks began to bulge. His eyes started to pop. He looked like a balloon about to burst.

Suddenly he could contain himself no longer.

"AWOL!!!!!" he roared. "AWOL!! They've gone AWOL!!!!!!"

"You mean they're not coming back?" asked Triv.

Kong's face changed to a deeper shade of purple.

"Five hundred lines, Trevellyan!" he raged. " 'I will not ask questions the headmaster cannot answer'!"

"You mean you don't know if they're coming back or not, sir?" Ingo chipped in. It was worth a few hundred lines to impress Susan Frost.

Ingo was in luck. Before Kong could respond, Susan Frost was posing a question of her own.

"What do you mean, 'AWOL', sir?" she asked sweetly.

Kong's face altered shape again, his voice softening to the level of a small tractor instead of a thirty-ton lorry grinding its way up the side of a hill.

"AWOL," he began to say, "is a military abbreviation. It stands for . . ."

Triv couldn't help himself. "Absent WithOut Leave," he called out.

Kong stopped. He thought of a number. A big number. He doubled it, added a couple of noughts and then doubled it again.

He took a deep breath.

" 'I will not interrupt my headmaster by saying that AWOL stands for Absent WithOut Leave, knowing jolly well that when this term is used in military circles it suggests that the person or persons to whom this term appertains are guilty

15

of leaving their posts and their responsibilities and their duties and everything else to their poor suffering commanding officer to sort out while they just disappear without a by-your-leave or a do-you-mind, leaving behind stupid notes and nothing else so that all their commanding officer has got to say is that they're ... they're ... deserters'!!!"

# 3

# Bubbles and burgers

"I want you . . ."

Triv blinked and looked again. And again, to confirm that his eyes weren't playing tricks on him.

They weren't. Not only was Susan Frost walking beside him – she was talking to him. To him! *To* him! To *him*!

"I want you . . ." she said again.

Moments ago, as he'd trudged out through the gates of St Ethelred's, Triv's spirits had been as heavy as his school bag. And his bag, stuffed with paper for writing Kong's lines, was megaheavy. But now those same spirits soared. He was wanted!

Triv smiled.

Susan Frost smiled, sort of.

Triv smiled again, a weak and sickly smile as it dawned on him that he didn't know what to say.

He racked his brains. Never mind James Trevellyan. How about James Bond? What did he usually say to women who said they wanted him?

"Pardon?" said Triv.

It was a pathetic effort and he knew it. But to have it overheard by someone else was even worse.

"Tee-hee-hee."

Triv recognized the little giggle at once. Only one person in the whole world made that noise. Susan Frost's best friend, Madeleine Mooney.

"Tee-hee-hee," went the giggle again. Not for nothing was Madeleine known throughout St Ethelred's as Mad Mooney.

Susan rescued Triv from his embarrassment. To his relief, he saw that she wasn't laughing at him.

"I want you," she said once more, "to explain what you said yesterday."

"Yesterday?" repeated Triv, parrot-like.

"When you said there was something fishy going on."

"Ah. Right. OK. Yes."

"Tee-hee-hee."

"Be quiet, Madeleine." Susan glared at her friend before switching her gaze back to Triv.

"Well," Triv began, "as I see it . . ."

Susan cut him short. "Not here," she said as a gaggle of first formers swept by hollering and hooting about what they hadn't done at school that day, "not in the *street*."

Triv had a flash of inspiration. He would take her for a meal. *That's* what James Bond would do.

"Let's go to the Wimpy Bar," he said, adding with what he hoped was a winning smile, "And the beefburgers are on me."

Susan's nose gave a disapproving little twitch. "Do they sell orange juice?" she asked. "Fresh orange juice?"

Of course, realized Triv with horror. The average beefburger was loaded with two hundred and eighty-three calories – not to mention a twenty-

18

one point three percent fat content. One did not attain the graceful poise of a Susan Frost by stuffing beefburgers with all the trimmings.

"Tee-hee-hee," Mad Mooney smiled at him. "Put me down for the beefy-burger, then. I'm feeling peckish."

Triv knew when he was beaten. If anybody deserved a spot in the record books it was Madeleine Mooney:

**World's most peculiar biological specimen**
*Madeleine Mooney of St Ethelred's School, who eats three square meals a day and dozens of round ones and still manages to look like a shoelace.*

"All right," sighed Triv.

He would claim it as a dinner date, and turn Ingo English green with envy. And he would conveniently forget to mention that Madeleine the Munchkin had been in tow.

"Orange juice it is, then," he said. "That's my kind of drink too."

"It is?" said Susan Frost.

"Sure is," said Triv, and gave her his James Bond look. "So long as it's shaken, not stirred."

\* \* \*

They found a table by the window. Susan, orange juice in hand, slid smoothly across the bench seat until she reached the glass.

Triv, carrying his own orange juice, was about to slide in next to her when his nerve failed. He took the seat opposite instead, excusing his cow-

19

ardice by telling himself that James Bond always sat opposite his women, too.

"Tee-hee-hee," giggled Madeleine Mooney, "thanks very much, Triv." She was carrying two beefburgers. They looked to Triv like scaled-down versions of St Paul's Cathedral.

"Any time," said Triv.

He shrugged nonchalantly and tried not to think about how much they'd cost him. He was rewarded by having Madeleine slide, not next to her friend Susan as he'd expected, but to him.

"I'll remember that," said Madeleine.

She was giving Triv a look of worrying friendliness, a look much as she might give to a double portion of chips.

Triv pretended not to notice. It wasn't that he didn't like Madeleine. As stair-rods went she was OK. It was just that everybody paled in comparison to Susan Frost.

He peered out of the window instead, to where the shopping precinct's ornamental fountain was bubbling and foaming.

"Somebody's put washing-up liquid in the fountain again."

"Pathetic," said Susan, glancing out of the window and then back again. "Quite pathetic."

She sipped her orange juice, puckering her lips in a way that made Triv feel weak at the knees.

"Well?" she said, suddenly businesslike.

"What?" said Triv. He had been concentrating on Susan's lips.

"Stitson and Co," said the lips. "What do you think it's all about?"

"Well..." Triv leant forward. "...it just seems funny to me..."

"Fishy, you said," interrupted Susan. "Fishy in what way?"

"It doesn't make sense," said Triv. "Take Miss Derbyshire for instance. She's never gone anywhere without her hat . . ."

"I'd never go anywhere with it," sniffed Susan.

"And then there's Stitson. He'd got everything ready for our metalwork class. Now why would he do that if he wasn't going to come back?"

"Well I don't know about him," said Susan. "But I'm quite certain about Mr Winkler. He would have told me if he'd known he wasn't going to be there for my piano lesson. I'm sure he would."

"Sudden decisions," murmured Triv. "Spur of the moment stuff. As though they'd had enough . . ."

"I haven't," said Madeleine from beside him. Beefburger number one had met its end.

"Madeleine, will you be quiet! This is serious."

"Tee-hee-hee."

Triv stared at Madeleine. A person who giggled when Susan Frost was being serious was either very brave or very stupid and Madeleine was neither of those. Very hungry, yes, but neither brave nor stupid.

And he was right. Madeleine was giggling at something else, something outside the window. As he turned to look for himself Triv saw that Susan was giggling as well now; an enchanting liquid giggle, he thought, like the sound of a tinkling waterfall.

At first he thought they were laughing at the ornamental fountain with its foaming suds. Until, that is, he saw what was really amusing them. Ingo English.

"Ingo, you twit," said Susan. She looked severe, but the words had a softness to them that made Triv's heart sink.

Ingo was standing just outside the window, all squashed lips and flattened nose as he pressed his face against the glass. Next to him, lips equally squashed and nose slightly more flattened, stood Watling. Triv noticed two things immediately.

One, that Watling's face wasn't pressed against the glass.

And two, as the pair of them hurried into the Wimpey Bar to join the party, that the bottle of washing-up liquid Ingo had in his hand was a "ten percent extra – FREE" offer, while Watling's was a Giant Economy size.

"Good, eh?" chuckled Ingo, plonking himself down beside Susan Frost and jerking a thumb in the direction of the foaming fountain.

There was only one word for it, thought Triv. The one Susan had used just a few moments before.

"Pathetic," he said.

Susan tutted. "Some people have no sense of humour," she said to Ingo.

"No sense of what?" asked Watling, squeezing himself on to the end of the seat and giving Ingo English the excuse to move even closer to Susan Frost.

"In your case, Watters," said Ingo, "just no sense."

Watling frowned, trying to think of something witty to hit back with. "Belt up," he said.

"So what're you three up to?" asked Ingo, "counting how many lines Triv's got to do by Monday?"

"Susan was asking me," Triv said, "what I thought about the missing teacher situation."

"Easy," said Ingo briskly. "Had enough of Kong, ain't they? They've all gone and pushed off somewhere else, where there's not so much hassle. Like the Foreign Legion."

Susan looked unaccountably impressed. "I can believe that."

Triv blinked. "What, old Mr Winkler yomping across the desert . . ."

"I mean I can believe they've all had enough of that dreadful man King as their headmaster," said Susan curtly. "I mean . . . the man's a complete Philistine."

Watling scratched his head. "I thought he come from Brighton."

"That piano duet was a farce," Susan went on. "It was supposed to be *Claire de Lune*."

"It came out half right then," said Triv, thinking it would be a good idea to cheer her up.

"What?"

"Not very Claire, but pretty loony."

The joke fell flat. Susan Frost gave Triv an icy stare. "Something must be done," she said. "Mr Winkler must return. My whole musical career depends on it."

"Count me in darling," said Ingo. "I wanna see Stitson back taking us for metalwork. Otherwise I ain't gonna finish me ashtray an' I'll have to buy my old man a Father's Day present."

"Yeah," grunted Watling. "Kong's geography's useless. He reckons Rome is the capital of Italy."

"Geb, I'b heb goo," said Madeleine Mooney through a mouthful of beefburger number two. It went down with a plug-hole gulp. "Yes, I'll help too," she repeated. "Mademoiselle Balmain was going to photocopy some Cordon Bleu recipes for me."

"Right," said Susan Frost firmly. "All the missing teachers sponsored my eight-hour Rachmaninov recital to raise funds for the Koala Bears in Need Appeal, so they all owe me money. I shall use that as an excuse to go round to their homes and tell them they must come back."

"Ask 'em, don't you mean?" said Ingo.

"No, tell. They have a duty."

"Fair enough," said Ingo keenly. "When do we start?" Roaming the town with Susan Frost was right up his street.

"Not we," said Susan. "I. This is something I have to do alone." She placed a hand on his. "But thanks for the offer, Ingo. And you, Madeleine. Even you, Watling. Yes, it's at times like this that one really discovers who one's true friends are."

Triv, who had been transfixed by the sight of Susan's snow-white hand landing on Ingo's grubby paw, suddenly realized that her frosty look was being directed at him.

"I would have thought that you, James, had more to gain than anybody. Unless you enjoy writing lines, that is?"

"No-o," said Triv hesitantly. "It's just that . . . well . . . if you reckon the teachers are staging an anti-Kong protest walk out . . . why didn't they all do it on the same day?"

"Because . . . because . . ." began Susan. She had no answer.

Ingo, ever the opportunist, leapt to the rescue. Attack was the best form of defence.

"All right, brainbox, what's your thinking?"

"Yeah," said Watling.

"Yes," said Madeleine Mooney, "tell us Triv." She started to chomp again.

"Yes, James," said Susan. "What *do* you think's happened to them, then?"

Triv gulped. He was on the spot. He opened his mouth and closed it again.

"Come on, spit it out," said Ingo.

"Yeah, spit it out," said Watling.

"Yeb," said Madeleine who, luckily, didn't spit it out.

"Well, James?"

Desperately, Triv resorted to his favourite school trick of looking out of the window for inspiration.

But all he saw was the ornamental fountain, still feeling the after-effects of the Ingo/Watling washing-up liquid attack.

The rising foam had risen as far as it could go and was now bubbling over the fountain's rim and down to a gaggle of children playing on the pavement below.

One little boy had really thrown himself into things and was covered from head to foot with creamy bubbles. Seeing him, the boy's mother screamed, plucked her child from the sea of foam and carried him off under her arm.

The scene made a thought flash through Triv's mind. Notes. All the teachers had left notes behind. And notes were suspicious, weren't they?

"Come on, we ain't got all day," jeered Ingo.

Watling had started singing. "Why are we waiting . . ."

Notes . . . who leaves notes? . . . the struggling kid being carted off against its will . . .

Before Triv knew it, the words had slipped out.

"Kidnapped!" he cried. "They've been kidnapped!"

Ingo laughed first, of course. A raucous hooting belly-laugh, loud and vulgar.

Madeleine Mooney followed, tee-hee-hee-ing and spraying the table with a cloud of breadcrumbs and beefburger.

Watling joined in then, trumpeting like an elephant with a wonky silencer. He slapped his thigh and stamped his foot for good measure.

And finally Susan laughed. A pealing, silvery laugh, which rang in Triv's ears and jangled around his head until all he could think was that he had to get away from it.

"I've got to be going now," said Triv, "things to do, and all that."

"Like half a billion lines," said Ingo English, to a further burst of laughter.

Dignity, thought Triv, leave with dignity. Politely, he said "excuse me" to Madeleine as he stepped past her and out into the aisle. "See you all on Monday."

"Not if we see you first," guffawed Watling, with more thigh-slapping and foot-stamping.

Dignity, Triv told himself again, leave with dignity. But even that wasn't going to be possible.

For, as he thigh-slapped, Watling accidentally knocked his giant economy bottle of washing-up liquid on to the floor. There, like Triv's blazer earlier that day, it found itself on the receiving end of Watling's size 9 foot-stamping.

The result was a pool of slippery stuff into which Triv, stepping boldly into the aisle, put both feet. The effect was dramatic.

He slithered forward, his legs cycling round like a cartoon cat, bounced off a couple of astonished senior citizens who had until that moment been enjoying a quiet salad, and knocked over a pile of trays.

His one moment of luck came as he was about to slither into the plate glass door. Somebody opened it.

Out Triv went, slowing at first, then accelerating again as he reached the smooth tiled surrounds of the ornamental fountain. With grace, if not dignity, he sailed on into the bubbles.

"Oh well," said Susan Frost cruelly, "at least he'll get his blazer clean."

# 4

# Triv in hiding

Mr Stitson's house had a red door and a collection of large rhododendron bushes in the garden.

By the time Susan Frost had pushed open the metalwork master's wrought-iron gate and glided up to the red door to rattle at its wrought-iron knocker, Triv had slipped through a gap in the wrought-iron fence and hidden himself in the largest of the rhododendron bushes. He yawned, quietly. He'd had a bad night.

Writing Kong's lines had taken him ages, what with having to wait for his stack of paper to dry out first. Even then the sheets still smelled of something that managed to clean dishes and yet be soft to your hands.

Then he'd lain awake half the night thinking about what a fool he'd been.

Kidnapped! What on earth had made him say a thing like that? Notes were sent by kidnappers, that was true. Ransom notes, asking for money. Not cheerio notes, written by the victims.

Yes, he'd made a fool of himself and there was only one thing to do. He had to redeem himself in some way, to win back a place in Susan's affections. But how?

He didn't know. But what he did know was that he had to be available for any chance that came up.

Which was how he came to be watching from the depths of one of Mr Stitson's rhododendron bushes as Susan Frost rattled yet again at the wrought-iron knocker. A vigorous rattle it was, full of determination.

But nobody answered.

\* \* \*

At Miss Derbyshire's house, things took a turn for the worse.

From the safety of his vantage point behind the huge oil tank which held the fuel for the chilly art mistress's central heating system, Triv watched helplessly as Susan was joined at Miss Derbyshire's front door by Ingo English.

"Thought I'd come along anyhow," Triv heard Ingo say. "Help with the old persuasion, like."

"That's nice of you, Ingo," said Susan Frost, a bit too warmly for Triv's liking. "I never have got on terribly well with Miss Derbyshire. In my view she has too high an opinion of Constable."

Triv's brain automatically pulled out facts. Constable. John. 1776–1837. Painter of English Landscapes.

His gloom lifted slightly as he heard Ingo say, "You and me both, Susie. I'm not keen on policemen meself."

Susan knocked once again at Miss Derbyshire's door.

No answer.

\* \* \*

Even from where he was hidden, between two bushy Highland Pines, Triv could hear Mr

29

McDougall's doorbell. Not a bell, in fact, but a chime.

Da-da di-da-da-da-da, da-da-di-da-da-da-da, da-da di-da-da-da-da da-da-di-daaaaaa . . .

Scotland the Brave, recognized Triv.

He chanced a quick look out from behind the smaller of the two conifers. Susan, her blonde hair flowing over her shoulders, was looking through the letterbox. So was Ingo English, clearly out to use every snuggling opportunity that came his way.

Susan pressed the bell-push and the tune bravely played again.

No answer.

* * *

At old Mr Winkler's bungalow Triv had a nasty moment which, as it happened, turned out quite well.

He had taken refuge in the middle of an overgrown hedge, watching unseen as Susan knocked at the door.

No answer.

Then he had watched as, with Ingo English breathing down her neck, she had looked through the letterbox. No sign.

It was as Susan Frost was peering through the lounge window, with Ingo doing his utmost to use the same square centimetre of glass, that it happened. From close by, Triv heard a rustling sound.

He held his breath, hoping he'd imagined it. He hadn't. He heard the sound again, closer this time.

Rustle, rustle.

Triv froze. Was somebody in the hedge with him?

Rustle. Rustle. Crunch.

Crunch? Leaves didn't go crunch. Crisps went crunch.

And crisp packets rustled, especially when they were being emptied by the grab-a-crisp-a-second arm action of Madeleine Mooney.

Triv was feeling happier by the minute. Ingo's look of dismay as the Mooney gooseberry walked into sight was one reason for this; and for another . . .

For another, the teachers might not have been kidnapped but they certainly seemed to have vanished into thin air.

Susan was turning away from Mr Winkler's door.

There'd been no answer.

\* \* \*

The garden at Mademoiselle Balmain's pied-à-terre was bare.

No bushy bushes for Triv to hide behind, just a wide expanse of lawn. No tall and dense surrounding hedge to bury himself in, either. The only decent hiding place was a forty-gallon rainwater barrel standing at the side of the house.

Triv waited until Susan, Madeleine and an unhappy-looking Ingo had walked up the short path to the front door. Then he scuttled along the narrow alleyway which separated the house from its neighbour, hopped over the low dividing fence and ducked down behind the barrel.

"She *must* be in," he heard Susan say.

"It looks empty," said Madeleine.

From behind the rainwater barrel, Triv couldn't tell if she meant the house or her crisp packet.

"You knock this time Madeleine," said Susan Frost. "You might bring us a change of luck."

"She's changed mine, that's for sure," muttered Ingo.

"Right-o," Triv heard Madeleine say. "Here goes."

What he heard next was confusing, to say the least. The noise was unlike any door knocker he'd ever heard.

Where he'd expected a sharp rat-a-tat sound, there came a metallic scraping. This was rapidly followed by a loud crash, a low rumbling, and finally a trio of angry voices.

"You berk!" yelled Ingo. "You great steaming berk!"

"Look at the *mess*," cried Susan.

"Yes, look." Madeleine paused before adding, "Cheese and mushroom pizza."

Triv couldn't resist it. He popped his head above the rainwater barrel and everything became clear.

The cheese and mushroom pizza Madeleine Mooney had been referring to was actually an empty packet just starting to perform cartwheels across the lawn.

But it was just part of the mess Susan had cried out about. The rest of it was cascading out of the dustbin now rolling noisily along the path, away from the person Ingo had called a berk. The person now slowly getting to his feet.

"Who you calling a berk?" said Watling.

"You," yelled Ingo.

"It weren't my fault. Stupid place to stick a dustbin if you ask me."

"Under your feet. Yeah, real stupid. I was wrong, Watters. You're not a great steaming berk. You're a great steaming, galloping multi-berk . . ."

Susan Frost cut the debate short. "Do you mind if we leave the question of how big a berk he is until later," she said sarcastically, "and clear that lot up?"

She waved a royal finger at the garden, which was now looking like a Council rubbish tip.

"Come on, then!" she ordered, her voice at its most commanding, "before it blows everywhere. Look in all the corners. I want every last scrap picked up."

"All right, Boadicea," grumbled Ingo.

"Yeh, all right, Boadicea," echoed Watling, "whoever he was."

Even Triv found himself obeying the order and picking up a small brown envelope that had blown across the garden to get stuck between the rain-water barrel and the wall. It had Mademoiselle Balmain's name and address on it, he noticed, neatly typed beneath a large red postmark and slogan.

He watched for a couple of minutes longer, most of which time Watling spent trying to pick up a carrier bag that he was kneeling on. Triv was almost happy.

From Watling's initial attempt to boot the dust-bin into orbit through to their final cleaning-up operation, they'd made enough noise to wake the dead. But nobody had appeared. Mademoiselle Balmain wasn't around either. Whatever the answer to this mystery was, his kidnapping theory no longer looked quite so daft.

Slipping the brown envelope into his pocket, he left the scene of the grime.

\* \* \*

Had he stayed a little longer, Triv's happiness would have been short-lived.

Not because Mademoiselle Balmain appeared; she didn't.

But because he would have heard Susan apologize to Ingo for her snappiness and been made depressed by seeing them leave the garden hand-in-hand.

He would also have seen Watling's attempt to put his arm round Madeleine's waist. That would have been the most depressing part of all.

"Do you mind, Watling?" Triv would have heard her cry, brushing Watling's hand away as though it were a crumb left over from lunch. "I am spoken for. James Trevellyan and I are going steady."

# 5

# Something's brewing

"I'm cold," muttered Miss Derbyshire. She wrapped her fur coat tightly about herself and shivered.

"Och," grunted Mr McDougall, "You dinna ken what cold is. Take yourself awa' for a nicht in the Caingorms, with the wind whistling up your kilt . . . then you'll ken aboot cold."

Miss Derbyshire looked at him bleakly. "I didn't bring my hat," she said. "Heat escapes from one's head."

"You ken that, don't you, Alex?" said Mr Stitson to the Scotsman. "You've enough hot air escaping from yours."

"Bah," replied Mr McDougall.

"Mind you," said Mr Stitson, "this place could be warmer. If I'd known we were coming here, I'd have brought along my portable furnace."

"Music is a good warming influence," said Mr Winkler, to nobody in particular. "It gives you an inner glow . . ."

"Prefer porridge myself," said Mr McDougall.

"Porreege?" said Mademoiselle Balmain, "what ees thees porreege?"

The question was to remain unanswered.

As Mr McDougall opened his mouth to reply, a familiar-sounding bell started to ring. Immediately, he closed his mouth and stood up.

Mademoiselle Balmain didn't pursue her porridge point, but got to her feet as well.

Mr Stitson stood up.

Miss Derbyshire stood up.

Slowly, but as immediately as he could manage, old Mr Winkler stood up.

They left the room and began to walk along a gloomy corridor. They walked – apart from the echoing of their footsteps and the creaking of Mr Winkler's bones – in complete silence.

Nobody spoke; not even to say how the gloominess of the corridor reminded them of St Ethelred's.

Neither, when they entered it moments later, did anybody say how much the room at the end of the corridor looked just like St Ethelred's staffroom.

Each of them simply sat down at one of the familiar-looking chairs grouped around the large familiar-looking table.

In front of them stood five familiar-looking receptacles, wisps of steam curling idly upwards from the brown liquid inside.

"Concoction 3 . . ." said a voice which sounded like a Dalek with a cold.

It came from the only thing about the room that was different from the layout of the St Ethelred's staff-room: an oblong loudspeaker which hung from one corner of the ceiling.

". . . Test 17," the voice continued.

Each of the teachers stretched out a hand.

Mr Stitson picked up the mug in front of him. It looked familiar. A vague and fuzzy memory swam into his mind, a memory of his retrieving this same mug from the staff-room at St Ethelred's just before he left.

The other teachers were experiencing the same sensation.

Mr McDougall, as he lifted his "Scotland the Brave" World Cup 1982 commemorative mug; Miss Derbyshire, wrapping both hands round her mug for warmth; Mr Winkler, reaching out for the same cup and matching saucer he'd been using every day for the best part of thirty years; Mademoiselle Balmain as she elegantly held her bone-china cup with her little finger extended – each felt the same.

"Drink!" commanded the tinny voice.

The teachers did as they were told. Only Mr Winkler's rattling cup and Mr Stitson's slurp broke the silence.

"Members of the Jury," said the voice when the five had finished. "Your points out of ten. Tester A?"

"One," grimaced Mr Stitson.

"Tester B?"

"One-and-a-half," said Miss Derbyshire. "It was nice and hot," she added.

"Tester C?"

"Terrible," growled Mr McDougall.

"A numerical value, Tester C."

"Och, one. No more."

"Tester D?"

"Only two," said Mr Winkler. "Sorry."

"Tester E?"

Mademoiselle Balmain stayed silent.

"Tester E?" repeated the voice. "Your points out of ten?"

"Nul point," said Mademoiselle Balmain determinedly. "No points."

From the loudspeaker came a sharp intake of breath. "You didn't like it, then?" crackled the voice.

For perhaps the first time ever, all five of the St Ethelred's teachers were in full agreement.

"Uggh!" they said together.

\* \* \*

Hidden in the room next door, a man sat at a microphone. He looked thoughtful. Beside him sat a woman. She looked thoughtful as well. They looked at each other.

"Is it the tea?" said the man.

"Or is it them?" said the woman.

"They're teachers. They're always drinking tea. They're experts, ain't they? If they're saying the tea leaves a lot to be desired, then it does."

"What does?"

"The tea leaves. A lot to be desired."

"What?"

"The tea leaves the tea leaves. It leaves a lot to be desired."

The woman shook her head. "That's what *they* say."

"That's what I said."

"No, no, no. What I'm saying is . . . forget the tea leaves. It could be them."

"Them?"

"Them. The jury."

"You could be right . . ." said the man thoughtfully. "Yes, a jury needs a judge, don't it? Someone to give it a bit of direction."

"Right."

"But we don't want a judge. We want a teacher. 'Cos teachers know about tea."

"We want a teacher what's like a judge."

"Someone with a bit of authority . . ."

"Right," said the woman.

"Someone like . . . yes!"

"Like what, Charlie?" asked the woman.

"Like a *headmaster*," said the man.

"Right!" said the woman.

"Come on then," said the man. He pulled out a small brown envelope and began typing a name and address on it. "We'll just catch the post."

# 6

# Just the ticket

Kong's study was like the man himself: large, forbidding and a long way up in the air. On the fourth floor, to be exact.

Triv had fought his way up three and a half of the four flights of stairs when he met the man himself coming down.

"Where are you going, Trevellyan?"

Triv looked up as far as he could without toppling backwards. He found himself addressing the second button of his headmaster's waistcoat.

"To your study, sir," he said. "To see you."

"Then you're out of luck."

"Why, sir?"

"Because I'm not there. There I am not. At least," the waistcoat button continued cheerily, "I wasn't when I left."

Triv couldn't understand it. If it had been anybody else, he would have said they were joking. But Kong in a good mood? It was like Madeleine Mooney saying no to a cream doughnut. Unheard of.

"Can I give me a message?" said Kong.

"Lines," said Triv, bemused.

"Lines, Trevellyan? Railway, tram, straight, life, head . . . what sort of lines?"

"The lines you set me on Friday," said Triv. He held up his bulging case.

"Smell like washing lines to me," said Kong as the aroma of bubbles wafted up towards him. "Deposit them on my desk."

Triv stepped to one side and walked up. Kong stepped to the same side and walked down. Triv stepped back to the side he'd started from. So did Kong. Back went Triv. Back went Kong. Triv moved. Kong moved. Triv went to move again, but this time found himself strangely rooted to the spot. Kong's mighty hand, gripping his shoulder like an iron clamp, had a lot to do with it.

"Six billion lines, Trevellyan," growled Kong. " 'I will not impersonate an obstacle course on the stairway . . .' "

"But . . ."

"Only jesting, Trevellyan," smiled Kong as he went by. And, as if that wasn't unbelievable enough, as he passed by at eye-level he actually winked. Winked!

Triv, shaking his head in disbelief at this amazing change in character, headed on up the stairs and into Kong's study.

It didn't take Triv long to find the desk that Kong had told him to leave his lines on. The thing was massive. Standing slap-bang in the centre of the room, it was like a snooker table without pockets.

It was also almost completely covered in junk. On one side there were piles of lines, pens, piles of lines, folders, piles of lines, an in-tray, piles of lines, an out-tray, and piles of lines. The other side was a little less cluttered. It just had piles of lines.

Looking for somewhere to leave his own stack

of paper Triv spotted a small, almost vacant, space just right of centre. It was occupied only by a small brown envelope, an envelope with Kong's name and address typed neatly on the front.

Triv lifted the envelope and plonked down his pile of lines. He was about to put the envelope back on top, so that Kong wouldn't miss it, when something caught his eye.

Alongside the first-class stamp was a slogan. It read, "Come On Round To The Globe".

Triv tiptoed to the door and checked outside. An eerie silence had descended, the sort of silence which meant either the end of the world or the start of registration. Assuming it wasn't the end of the world, he crept back to Kong's desk.

Gently he opened the envelope. It contained a ticket.

### OLDE TYME MUSIC HALL
*Row E, Seat 11*
*Performance commences at 8pm*

Across it was stamped a date. Tonight's performance, realized Triv.

Triv turned the ticket over and suddenly saw why Kong had been in such a good mood. Somebody had written on the back, "With the compliments of the Globe Theatre". Kong had been sent a free ticket to the theatre.

But that wasn't what intrigued him. It was the "Come On Round To The Globe" postmark on the front.

Hurriedly, Triv checked his pockets. He pulled out two dozen picture cards, a *Fascinating Facts*

42

*and Figures* book and a bus timetable before he found what he was looking for.

The envelope he'd picked up when he was hiding behind Mademoiselle Balmain's rainwater barrel. The envelope that had come from her dustbin.

He laid it on the desk, beside Kong's envelope. The similarities struck him immediately.

Mademoiselle Balmain's envelope had her name and address typed neatly on the front; so did Kong's.

Her envelope had been posted first class; so had Kong's.

And Mademoiselle Balmain's envelope also had a postmark. "Come On Round To The Globe," it said.

\* \* \*

"Hello ducks."

Triv looked at the woman. Sitting behind the small grille of the Globe Theatre box office, she looked like something out of an old Knights-of-the-Round-Table film, a damsel in distress trapped in a castle turret.

"Wanna ticket?" the woman enquired. She had a bright red face. More of a damson than a damsel.

"No, not really." said Triv. "I just wanted some details about the show."

"Oooh, it's a good show ducks. I watch it every night." The woman thrust a paw out of her cage. Triv took the glossy leaflet that she was offering. "There y'are, that's who's on."

Triv looked at the leaflet. It had *Olde Tyme Music Hall* across the top and a collection of photographs beneath.

"Monday night is bargain night," said the woman.

"Sorry?" said Triv. He had been looking at the list of artistes. Happy Harry Harmer, The Humming Humourist. Belinda Browning, the Voice of Song. The Zwrickilizocki Troupe, International Acrobats.

"Buy one ticket, get another one half-price," the red face said. "Special for Mondays. Mondays are slow, see."

"I don't think so," said Triv, still looking at the glossy leaflet, although he wasn't sure exactly what for.

The woman carried on regardless. "Helps bump up the audience see, special offers like this one. Your top artistes, they don't like doing their stuff to rows of empty seats. They need the right mood, see, else they get in a right mood."

"No thanks," said Triv, "no, I don't . . ."

Then he spotted it. The photograph of a bearded man, down in one corner of the leaflet.

". . . yes, I will. One please."

"Gooood!" Above the sill of her little window the woman's red face glowed with pleasure. "Where d'you wanna sit?" She swivelled a seating plan round so Triv could see it.

"Row F, Seat 11," said Triv instantly.

"Oooh, that's what I like. An instant precision."

It had been an easy choice. Kong's free seat was Row E, Seat 11. Triv would be right behind him.

"How about another one?" said the woman. "Half price on Mondays, remember. Good-looking young man like you must have loads of pretty young ladies he can pick from."

Triv hesitated. Could he? Should he?

44

He didn't want to make a fool of himself again. He studied the leaflet once more. The bearded man stared back at him with piercing eyes.

"The Great Wallendo," read the words beneath the face. "Hypnotist Extraordinaire."

If Kong and Mademoiselle Balmain had been sent free tickets for this show perhaps they all had.

The disappearing teachers hadn't been kidnapped.

They'd been hypnotized!

Yes, The Great Wallendo was the key to everything, Triv was sure of that. But sure enough to ask Susan Frost along as a witness? No, he was not.

But, the other side of Triv's brain argued, if by some chance you're wrong, just don't say anything. Nothing's lost and you've recovered ground with the divine Susan at half price.

He looked again at the leaflet, and another act on the bill. Georgi Stostakovich, he noticed. Classical Pianist from Russia. Perfect. He would offer Susan Frost a night out at the theatre and some enchanting piano music. He would solve the missing teachers mystery, become a hero of the school and all would be fine.

"Right. Two tickets it is then. Row F, Seats 11 and 12," he said with a lot of precision.

\* \* \*

"VIBGYOR."

Ingo English looked at Triv in a peculiar way. "Who's he when he's at home?"

"VIBGYOR," repeated Triv. "Violet, Indigo,

45

Blue, Green, Yellow, Orange, Red. The colours of the rainbow."

"Sounds more like the Rumanian goalie," muttered Ingo.

He wandered back across the laboratory to where his partner Watling was looking down the tube of a bunsen burner so that he could see where the flame came from when he lit it.

Triv breathed a sigh of relief. He'd been unable to get Susan on her own since lunch and now it was Physics, the last period of the day.

Ingo would be hanging around her when school ended, that was certain. So if he was going to ask her to come with him to the Globe Theatre, it was now or never.

Now, he decided.

They'd been experimenting with light, taking it in turns to go into the tiny darkroom at the back of the lab and shine a beam through a glass prism to see how it split into the colours of the rainbow.

Looking to where Susan had been sitting, Triv saw an empty spot. He hadn't seen her move, but the conclusion was obvious: she was in the darkroom. It was the chance he'd been waiting for.

He strolled nonchalantly to the darkroom door and knocked gently. "Susan," he whispered.

Inside he thought he heard the scrape of a chair on the floor.

"Would you like to come out with me tonight?" whispered Triv.

"What?" came the muffled reply from the darkroom.

"I said . . ." hissed Triv. He glanced around to

make sure that nobody was listening. ". . . would you come out with me tonight. To the theatre."

"Mmmm."

Triv couldn't work out whether the answer was yes or no. "Was that 'yes'?" he whispered.

"Mmmmm."

"Pardon?" hissed Triv, a little louder this time.

"Mmmmmmmm."

This was becoming irritating. Triv forgot himself and raised his voice to normal volume; if anything, slightly greater than normal volume. "Yes or no?" he called.

"Yes," came a cool voice from behind him. Triv turned round, slowly. Behind him, Susan Frost was smiling. "I'm sure she would. Romeo."

"Sure she would," crowed Ingo English, "Casanova."

"Yeah," called Watling, "Canasova . . . Cavanosa . . . Navasoca . . ." He gave up. "Loverboy."

Triv felt himself blushing. Behind Susan, behind Ingo and Watling, every other face in the room was now looking his way. Correction: not *every* other face. One face was missing.

Triv turned again as the darkroom door creaked open. A hand emerged holding a half-eaten slice of buttered toast. Then the missing face, chomping on the bitten half.

"Yeb I bould," said Madeleine Mooney. "Gweetheart."

# 7

# There's no business like showbusiness

Outside the Globe Theatre, Triv looked at his watch. Seven fifty-eight.

From inside he heard a crash of cymbals, then a round of applause. Triv looked at his watch again. Seven fifty-nine. Where was she?

Being stuck with Madeleine was bad enough, but missing The Great Wallendo as well would be too bad.

Then he saw her, getting off a bus on the other side of the road. She had a carrier bag under her arm.

"Sorry, I'm late," she called as she crossed the road, "I had to go to the supermarket first."

The cymbals crashed again. "Come on," said Triv, "It's starting." He moved towards the main doors.

"Aren't you going to offer to carry my bag?" said Madeleine. "Gentlemen do that sort of thing."

Triv reluctantly took the bulging bag from her.

"Just a little something in case we get peckish during the show," said Madeleine. "Darling."

\* \* \*

By the time they got inside the lights were down and the first act, a high-kicking chorus line, had started.

Triv led the way down the centre aisle. His eyes

were still not accustomed to the dark by the time they reached row F. This, plus the weight of Madeleine Mooney's carrier bag, made groping along the row doubly difficult.

"Aaagh!" said somebody as Triv stood on their toe.

"Ouch!" said somebody else as he clouted a knee with the carrier bag.

Some of the heads sitting in row E swung round to find out what the fuss was all about. One bullet-shaped head in particular began to turn. The head of St Ethelred's head.

Suddenly a roll of drums came from the orchestra pit. Kong turned back towards the stage and Triv dived into his seat with a sigh of relief.

The last thing he wanted was for Kong to know he was there. Something was going to happen tonight, Triv could feel it in his bones. He watched and waited.

Belinda Browning (The Voice of Song) came, warbled her way happily through some songs, and went.

From where Triv was sitting, her act had been accompanied by two quite different sounds.

Immediately in front of him, Kong had been humming along with all the musical charm of a dentist's drill.

And from his right, Madeleine had started to work her way through the contents of the carrier bag.

A slab of fruit and nut chocolate went during Belinda Browning's first song, a carton of pineapple juice during the second, and her encore, fittingly, saw Madeleine polish off another chocolate bar.

Arbuthnot Andrews (Juggler of Wellington Boots and Other Items That Most People Don't Juggle With) came and went, lasting as long as a cornish pastie.

The Zwrickilizocki Troupe, overrunning by ten minutes when the youngest Zwrickilizocki sneezed and caused their human pyramid to collapse, gave Madeleine Mooney the chance to munch her way through a titanic bag of salt and vinegar crisps.

Then, as the Zwrickilizocki Troupers carried each other offstage to a sympathetic round of applause, Triv heard her whisper in his ear.

"Want a marshmallow?"

Madeleine's latest dip into her carrier bag had produced a huge round box of creamy white marshmallows, complete with a sharp-pronged wooden fork. She had speared one and was waving it in his direction.

"No, thanks," said Triv.

"Up to you, sweetykins," said Madeleine, and swallowed the marshmallow with a gulp.

"Lad-ies and Gentle-men!" The voice of the compere, a whiskery individual on a rostrum by the side of the stage, rang round the theatre. "The act you are a-bout to see is tru-ly a-mazing! A perf-form-er with a-mazing pow-er!"

"You're sure you don't want one?" whispered Madeleine. She'd pronged another dollop of squashy marshmallow with the wooden fork and was waving it under his nose again.

"I'm sure," hissed Triv.

"You haven't eaten a thing," murmured Madeleine. "And I went to the supermarket specially."

"Later," said Triv. He heard the second marshmallow go the same way as the first in spite of the compere building his introduction up to fever pitch.

"Intro-ducing! For your en-joy-ment! The man of mys-tery! The man of pow-er! The man who can make things hap-pen what you don't want to hap-pen! The . . ."

Triv held his breath as the master of ceremonies paused to consult his notes.

"The . . . Great Wallendo!!"

The big build-up had done the trick. The bearded man from the glossy brochure marched on to the stage to a tremendous round of applause.

Only two people didn't join in.

One, because she was poking a fork into a mar-shmallow and she couldn't clap with one hand.

And the other, Triv realized, because he was asleep.

It had seemed strange that, since humming tunelessly along with Belinda Browning (The Voice of Song), Kong had been quiet. He hadn't applauded any of the acts. He hadn't even joined in the laughter when the Zwrickilizocki Troupe's human pyramid collapsed.

Now, as the headmaster of St Ethelred's gave a grunt and shifted to a more comfortable pos-ition, Triv knew why. Kong began to make the dentist's drill sound again. He hadn't been hum-ming along with Belinda Browning (The Voice of Song) at all, realized Triv. He'd been snoring.

Up on stage, The Great Wallendo was starting his act. "Thank you, thank you," he boomed. "Now, I need a member of the audience to help me."

Kong snored on.

"Somebody not easily fooled," said The Great Wallendo, peering out into the darkness. "A sensible and sober member of society. A teacher, say." The man's black beard divided in two, revealing a thin and sinister smile. "Is there a teacher in the house?"

"Wob bid he bay?" marshmallowed Madeleine.

"Teacher," murmured Triv. "He wants a teacher to come up on stage."

"Any teachers in the audience?" asked The Great Wallendo again.

Kong snored on.

"No teachers?" boomed The Great Wallendo. "None at all?"

Triv's mind whirled.

If The Great Wallendo was asking for a teacher now, then maybe he'd been doing the same thing all along. And if he was right, that Mademoiselle Balmain's envelope from the Globe Theatre had also had a free ticket in it and that all the others had received free tickets as well, then . . . then maybe every one of them had been the victim of whatever it was that The Great Wallendo did in his act. That would explain it! Some unfortunate side effect had caused them to forget what they were, where they lived and so on. Or else . . .

"No teacher at all?" asked the bearded man on the stage.

. . . Or else it wasn't a side effect. Not an accident at all. They'd been put under the influence for a reason.

"Not even . . . a headmaster?"

The Great Wallendo peered out into the auditorium again. This time, though, it seemed to Triv that he was looking at one seat in particular. At seat 11 in Row E.

The occupant of that seat snored on.

"No teachers," said The Great Wallendo. "Oh dear."

It came to Triv in a flash. They *had* been kidnapped! Not by force, but by hypnotism! And Kong was the next victim! Which meant ... what? Which meant that if Kong got himself hypnotized as well he'd turn up at St Ethelred's tomorrow morning, all ready to shoot off at lunchtime. And knowing that, Triv would be ready to follow him. He'd be able to find out where the other teachers were, get them back again, Kong could return to being what he was before he became the scourge of 3B, and he, James Trevellyan, would be the hero of the hour!

"Oh dear, oh dear. No teacher in the house." The Great Wallendo was shaking his head sadly. "Oh dear."

*Snore*, snored Kong. *Grunt*, grunted Kong.

Triv was getting desperate. Everything depended on Kong getting himself hypnotized. And, by the look of it, that wasn't going to happen. Not unless the snoring, grunting Kong woke up.

The answer to Triv's prayers came from a most unexpected quarter.

"Goo wob dis bun?" said Madeleine Mooney.

The fact that she was showing the depth of her feeling for him by offering him the last marshmallow in the box was lost on Triv.

His reaction was immediate and, frankly, lacking in good manners.

He snatched the fork from her.

He thrust the marshmallow in his mouth.

And thrust the fork into Kong's backside.

The Great Wallendo's voice rose from despair to hope in one sentence.

"Not a single teach. . .ah!!!"

Kong, with a wail of agony that the rest of the audience took to be enthusiasm, had leapt to his feet.

"Yes we have!" yelled The Great Wallendo.

A wave of applause swept the theatre as a pair of spot-lights converged on Kong. Clutching the seat of his trousers as though they were on fire he whirled round to see Triv, still holding the incriminating marshmallow fork.

"Come on down!" The Great Wallendo was shouting, "Have I got a surprise for you!"

Kong grimaced. His eyes darted from left to right as the people around him shouted and pointed towards the stage. Then he was gone, his final words leaving Triv without much doubt about his feelings.

"Not," he howled, "as big as the surprise that's coming to you, Trevellyan!"

# 8

# Kong in the spotlight

"And your name is?" asked The Great Wallendo.

"King," growled Kong.

"Good to meet you, Mr King. And your first name?"

Kong mumbled something which Triv didn't catch. Neither did anybody else, including The Great Wallendo.

"A little louder, Mr King. I'm not sure everybody heard that."

"Cedric," said Kong through clenched teeth.

"Cedric. What a good name! Welcome, Cedric! Take a seat!"

The Great Wallendo led Kong towards a chair. Kong sat down slowly, wincing as he landed on the puncture Triv's fork had made.

"Ladies and gentlemen, a round of applause for our good friend Cedric, if you please!"

The audience, anticipating some fun, clapped and cheered before settling down again.

Back in row F, Madeleine Mooney was thoroughly confused. "What's Kong doing up there," she said. "And what's that man with the beard going to do?"

"He's going to hypnotize him," whispered Triv. "Like he did all the others."

"All the others who?"

"Ssshhh!" hissed somebody from a seat in the row behind them.

"The missing teachers," whispered Triv. "I reckon they were all given free tickets to see this show."

"But . . ." began Madeleine.

"And if I'm right, and they were, and this Great Wallendo called them up and hynotized them . . ."

"Ssssshhhhh!" came a chorus of ssssshhhhhs from the row behind.

"And it went wrong somehow . . . or right," Triv added with a sinister edge to his voice, "that is if it was meant to go wrong . . ."

"But . . ." tried Madeleine once more.

"Ssssshhhhhh!"

"And they all got put under the influence . . ." said Triv.

A hot and belligerent face leant forward from the seats behind. "If you two don't shut your gobs," it said, "you two will find yourselves under the influence of my boot."

"Ssssshhhhh!!"

"Wait and see," said Triv.

\* \* \*

Up on stage, Kong was looking a fraction happier as the pain in his backside eased a little.

"Cedric," the bearded man was saying, "tell the audience! Have we met before?"

"Not to my knowledge," answered Kong, "to my knowledge, not." He was starting to get the hang of stage talk as well.

The Great Wallendo nodded. At the same time he slid a medallion on a gold chain from his waist-coat pocket.

"And you are a teacher, Cedric?"

"A headmaster," corrected Kong with some pride.

"A headmaster!" boomed The Great Wallendo, encouraging the audience into another round of applause. He held the medallion in front of Kong's eyes and started to swing it to and fro.

"A position of very great responsibilitude," said Kong, staring at the glittering medallion.

"You give the orders, you mean?"

"Indeed," said Kong slowly. His eyes were revolving like marbles in a saucer. "Deed in."

"Cedric commands and the others jump!" boomed The Great Wallendo. "Is that right, Cedric?"

"Right to the point of exactitude!" said Kong. He was starting to enjoy this. "They jump all right!" He threw in a sound effect for good measure. "Boinggggggggg!"

The Great Wallendo swung the medallion a little faster. His tone changed. "You are feeling very sleepy, Cedric," he said quietly, "isn't that so?"

"Nope," said Kong.

"Cedric, I want you to take some orders from me."

"Nope."

"Cedric . . ."

"Nope, nope, nope," said Kong. "One cannot order Cedrics. Cedrics know what you're up to, see," he said, still goggling at the moving medallion. "And if you think a Cedric can be hypnotized by you pendulising a pendulisatory penduliser in front of his eyeballs then you've got another think com-"

57

"I am The Great Wallendo!"

The hypnotist, arms raised in triumph, had turned to face the audience.

Behind him Kong was staring blankly into space, his mouth open.

"This man is now putty in my hands!" The Great Wallendo's beard cracked in a smile. "My wish is his command!"

He turned back to Kong. St Ethelred's headmaster hadn't moved. His mouth was still giving its impression of the entrance to the Mersey Tunnel.

"Cedric," said The Great Wallendo gently, "can you hear me, Cedric?"

"Ye-es," moaned Kong.

"What is your name?"

"Cedric."

"No," said The Great Wallendo, shaking his head. "You're wrong. Your name isn't Cedric any more. Your name is Bonzo. You are a dog."

Kong's eyes flickered.

"What do you say to that . . . Bonzo?"

For a moment there was silence. Kong closed his mouth. He looked at The Great Wallendo with staring eyes. Slowly, his mouth came open again.

"Woof!" went Kong.

"Good boy, Bonzo!"

The audience broke into wild applause. The Great Wallendo held up a hand. Clearly there was more to come.

"Dogs do not sit on chairs, Bonzo. Off!"

Kong obeyed. He slipped from the chair and went down on to all fours.

"Woof!" he barked, cocking his head to one side. The Great Wallendo bent down and ruffled

58

Kong's hair. "Bonzo, you are a clever dog. Prove to the ladies and gentlemen that you are a clever dog. What is . . . one plus two?"

"Woof! Woof!" barked Kong. He paused, concentrating on the arithmetic. "Woof!"

"Well done, Bonzo!" beamed The Great Wallendo. "I think that deserves a reward. Don't you, ladies and gentlemen?"

As the audience laughed and applauded, the hypnotist dipped a hand into the pocket of his black jacket. Out came a rubber bone.

Kong's response was immediate. Looking adoringly at the rubber bone, he started panting.

"Ah-ah," chided the hypnotist. "Beg, Bonzo."

Kong went back on to his haunches. He pulled his arms into his sides and put the backs of his hands under his chin. Then, thinking that might not be enough, he opened his mouth and let his tongue flop out appealingly.

"What do we say, Bonzo?"

"Woof!"

"Anything else?"

"Howl!" howled Kong, "hooowwwllll!"

That was when The Great Wallendo made a very bad mistake. Instead of giving Kong/Bonzo the rubber bone to have a good gnaw on, he held it higher.

Kong's doggy face looked aggrieved. "Woof!" he barked. "Woooooooooooff!! Wooff! Hoowwwwllll! Wooff!!!"

He wanted that bone. He really wanted that bone. With an enormous bound, Kong leapt up from the floor and lunged for The Great Wallendo's hand.

The hypnotist didn't have a chance. In a flash,

Kong had knocked him to the ground and was climbing all over him.

"Get off, you brute! Get off!" yelled the hypnotist as Kong pinned him to the ground and started licking his face.

The audience was in hysterics. Half of them were crying with laughter. The other half were cheering Kong on.

"Sit!" screamed The Great Wallendo desperately.

Kong didn't want to sit. He wanted that rubber bone.

But begging hadn't worked. And licking his master's face hadn't worked.

This, his doggy mind concluded, called for different tactics.

"Woof! Woof! Howwll! Aariff! Ggggrrrrrrrrr!!"

With a giant lunge Kong sunk his teeth into The Great Wallendo's arm.

"Aaaaagggghhhhh!!" screamed The Great Wallendo.

"Grrrr! Chomp! Grrrr!" growled Kong.

"Sit! Aaa-gggh! Heel! Eeooooww!!"

The Great Wallendo was becoming desperate. Visions of being the only one-armed hypnotist in showbusiness swam before his eyes.

There was only one thing for it. He switched the rubber bone into his free hand. Then, summoning every ounce of strength that he could muster, The Great Wallendo whacked Kong behind the ear.

It did the trick.

Kong, alias Bonzo, loosened his grip. The hypnotist seized his chance and belted him again, this time on the back of the head. With a low moan, Kong keeled over.

The theatre was in uproar. People cheered and clapped, laughed and held their sides to stop them aching.

Back in row F, even Triv had temporarily forgotten why he'd wanted Kong to become the hypnotist's victim in the first place. Now though, as up on stage Kong rubbed his head and flopped back on to the chair, he remembered.

He watched carefully as, in the midst of the commotion, The Great Wallendo stared deep into Kong's eyes and said something to him. Kong nodded in agreement. The hypnotist said something else to him, then held all five fingers of his right hand in front of Kong's face.

Whatever it was The Great Wallendo was saying though, only Kong could hear. Not a sound was coming out through the loudspeaker system.

A few moments later The Great Wallendo, looking like a man who'd had an argument with a combine harvester, led Kong to the footlights.

"Ladies and gentlemen!" he boomed. "Your appreciation for Cedric King!"

Kong tottered down the short flight of steps at the side of the stage as The Great Wallendo joked without enthusiasm that, "he deserves a round of a-paws!"

And with that the hypnotist waved to the audience, gave what looked to Triv like a huge sigh of relief at having survived to hypnotize another day, and staggered slowly from the stage.

As the applause slowly died, the lights came up. People began to move, pushing out towards the foyer and the bar as the interval began.

"I enjoyed that," said Madeleine Mooney.

Triv didn't ask whether she meant The Great

Wallendo's performance or the contents of the now empty carrier bag on her lap. Something had just occurred to him.

"He turned it off!" he exclaimed.

"Turned what off?" asked Madeleine.

"His microphone!" said Triv. "Right at the end, when he was talking to Kong. He turned it off!"

He'd assumed that the hypnotist's microphone had been torn off in the struggle to save his arm. But that hadn't been the case. When he'd called for the audience to show their appreciation for Kong's antics, it had been working perfectly.

"Why would he do that?" asked Madeleine.

"It's obvious, isn't it? That was when he gave Kong his instructions!"

"What instructions?"

"I don't know what instructions," hissed Triv. "The same instructions he gave Stitson and the others, I suppose."

'But . . .'

"Instructions telling them to walk out . . ."

"But . . . you're wrong!" cried Madeleine, waving, for some reason best known to herself, the carrier bag.

It was Triv's turn to look blank. "What?"

"James . . . honeybun . . . I've been trying to tell you! I've seen them!"

"Wha . . . whe . . . ?" stammered Triv.

Madeleine Mooney was still waving the carrier bag in the air. In his confusion Triv vaguely noticed that its yellow surface proclaimed a message: "I shop at BBB's – for Bargain Buys in Bulk".

"Tonight," said Madeleine. "At the supermarket. They were all there. Mr Stitson, Miss Derbyshire, Mr McDougall, dear old Mr Winkler and

Mademoiselle Balmain. I saw them. Through a window behind the cheese counter. All of them!"

Before Triv could say anything, the lights went down again. Or so it seemed, as a large dark shadow fell across his seat. He looked up towards the stage. The curtain was still down.

"Trevellyan," growled the shadow.

Triv had no need to look up. He knew that growl well. He also knew that, whatever else he may have said, The Great Wallendo hadn't given Kong any instructions about being nice to schoolboys.

"You will be outside my study tomorrow lunchtime, boy," said Kong. "Without fail."

Triv waited for a message, together with a number with a lot of noughts on the end telling him how many times he'd got to write it out. The good news was that no such message came. The bad news was what came instead.

"And Trevellyan . . . you will be in your running gear."

# 9

# Triv on the run

Noon the next day found Triv sitting glumly in the boys' changing rooms.

"Keen, ain't he?" crowed Ingo English.

"Yeah," said Watling, bending one of the coat hooks so that it pointed downwards, "Keen as custard."

"Off for a run with Kong, eh?" jeered Ingo. "Doing a bit of crawling."

Triv gulped. Crawling was just what he would be doing by the time this was over.

Kong's lunchtime runs were legendary. At twelve-thirty on the dot St Ethelred's headmaster would hare out of the school gates, turn sharp left for the short burst to the playing field entrance, turn sharp left again as he reached it, then gallop across the field in a cloud of dust.

On the far side, where the boundary of the playing field met the municipal park, Kong would vault over the fence without stopping, do a dozen laps of the boating lake and still be back thirty minutes later.

"Come on then, what you waiting for?" goaded Ingo. "Get them legs moving, Trevellyan! Hup-two-three-four!"

Watling joined in the fun. "Yeah, come on! Hup-two-three-five . . ."

Triv moved.

"And marathon man is on the way!" commented Ingo English into a make-believe microphone.

"Mara-thon! Mara-thon!" chanted Watling.

The reminder didn't help Triv feel any better as he trudged out through the changing room door and into the corridor. It made him think about Pheidippides.

Not about the fact that good old Pheidippides had run twenty-six miles and three hundred and eighty-five yards non-stop, bringing the latest scores in a battle between the Persians and the Greeks taking place on the Plain of Marathon, and so invented the famous race.

No. More about the fact that, having done so, good old Pheidippides had dropped dead.

And then Triv heard the cheering.

At first he thought it was coming from outside, but as he drew nearer to the stairs he noticed that the route up to Kong's study was lined with faces he recognized. And all of them were cheering. Cheering him!

As he mounted the stairs, hands clapped him on the back. The cheering grew louder with every step so that, for one minute, he imagined himself as the runner who turns up with the torch to light the Olympic flame.

He looked upwards and the dream faded. At the top of the stairs there was no spherical shape waiting for him. Quite the opposite, in fact. A straight shape was waiting for him. The straight shape of Madeleine Mooney.

"My hero!" she sang.

"Madeleine has been telling us all about your evening out," said Susan Frost, shimmering into view.

Triv's heart sank. "Oh," he said.

"And about what you did. I'm impressed."

"He was wonderful," sighed Madeleine.

"Yes. I'm inclined to agree." Susan was smiling. Not laughing this time, but really smiling.

"You are?"

"Oh, yes!" said Susan.

"Everyone wants our teachers back again," Madeleine Mooney said. "But you're the only one who's tried to do anything about it! We all think you're wonderful."

The ranks lining the stairs broke into another burst of cheering.

"We've all had enough of Kong too," said Susan Frost. "And your attempt at incapacitating him was so original and brave. I mean, a marshmallow fork!"

Triv shrugged in an it-was-nothing sort of way.

"Such a pity it wasn't a garden fork," the angelic Susan went on, "but there we are. And in the end, it was all for nothing."

"I told Susan I'd seen them," said Madeleine. "Mr Stitson and the others. At the supermarket."

"Obviously they've gained alternative employment," said Susan, "although how spending the day with tons of food can compare with being here, I don't know."

Madeleine looked as though she did, but said nothing.

"So that's it. I will, of course," said Susan coldly, "be going out there straight after school." She sounded like a resistance fighter who'd just discovered she'd been betrayed to the enemy. "If nothing else, I can give them a piece of my mind."

"Yeah," said Watling who, along with Ingo English, had followed Triv up the stairs. "I'll come with you. They can have a piece of my mind and all."

"Leave it out, Watters," said Ingo. "That wouldn't leave any for you."

Susan Frost's amber eyes flashed angrily. "Very witty Ingo," she said tartly. "But then that's your style, isn't it? Picking on those who can't defend themselves. But when it comes to real danger, where are you? Nowhere."

She took a step closer to Triv. "Well, let me tell you," she said, "I like men who are men."

And with that she bent and kissed Triv on the cheek. "It is a far, far better thing you do now than you have ever done before," she said dramatically.

*Tale of Two Cities*, thought Triv. Not quite right, but close enough to send shivers down his spine.

"My hero," said Madeleine again and kissed him on the other cheek.

"I agree," said Susan Frost with another withering look at Ingo English. "Such bravery! It simply takes your breath away."

A sharp rat-a-tat of footwear stopped the chatter dead. Turning in its direction, they saw Kong. He had emerged from his office, dressed in a vivid orange track-suit, and was running on the spot. He looked like a pneumatic carrot.

"Then you'll soon have some company, young lady," growled Kong. "Because awayness of breath is what you, Trevellyan, are soon going to find you've got."

\* \* \*

And he was right. Triv was soon gasping.

His lungs felt as though they'd been used by a trainee fire-eater. His legs ached, and his side had more stitches in it than an elephant's cardigan.

They'd got as far as the school gates.

"You're not fit, Trevellyan," bawled Kong, still running on the spot. "That's the trouble with the youth of today. No backbone."

Triv wasn't going to argue. He couldn't feel his backbone. He couldn't feel any bone, for that matter.

"Wagons-ho!" cried Kong and galloped away.

Triv followed. He staggered down the road, limped left at the entrance to the school playing fields and hobbled across to the boundary fence where Kong was waiting impatiently.

"Are we suffering, Trevellyan?" beamed Kong.

If he'd had the energy, Triv would have nodded. Instead he simply fell down.

Kong's strong hands helped him up. And up. And up, until he was level with the top of the fence. Then they threw him over.

"On your feet, Trevellyan!" said Kong, vaulting over the fence to drop down beside him. "Recuperization comes later."

Triv staggered to his feet. "How much later?"

"Not much," said Kong cheerily as he bounded away again, hauling Triv along by his shirt. "Four miles or so."

* * *

A curious duck eyed Triv suspiciously as he lay wheezing for breath beside the pond.

Nearby, Kong was doing press-ups on the grass. So was Triv's heart, or at least that was how it felt. He'd lost count of how many times Kong had

68

dragged him round the duckpond before he'd been allowed to collapse in a heap.

"Dearie me, Trevellyan," Kong said. "What's up?"

"I can't go on," moaned Triv.

Kong looked down. "Nonsense, laddie. Go through the pain barrier, that's all you need to do."

"I have. It was painful."

"Bah!" said Kong. "It's just a mental deficiency. Mind over matter, that's what it's all about. Think alternative thoughts! Give that brain of yours something else to think about. Keep it cerebral-isating and it won't have time to tell the rest of your bits they're not enjoying life."

Triv closed his eyes. "Sorry, sir. The rest of my bits are telling my brain they're not going to move."

"And I," growled Kong, "am telling 'em they are. So on your feet!"

Triv managed to heave himself on to his knees. He tried to think, to think of anything to take his mind off the torture still to come. He failed. The only thing he could manage was an epitaph for his tombstone:

> James "Triv" Trevellyan
> (1978–1992)
> He suffered bravely,
> a doughty fighter;
> When his body fell
> 'twas a kilo lighter.

"Snap into it Trevellyan!" snarled Kong.
Triv had the feeling that snap was just about

all his legs could do now. He had managed to stagger on to his feet but that was as far as his legs seemed prepared to go.

"It's my legs!" he moaned. "They won't move!"

"Make them."

"I can't. They've gone on strike."

Kong smiled menacingly. "Strike. What a good idea." He looked around. "There must be something I can find to strike you with, Trevellyan, if that's what it takes."

Triv staggered a couple of steps.

"Good! Good!" Kong had found a whippy branch with an ominously pointed end. "Off we go then. Any flagging, and you get a flogging. We're late enough as it is."

He looked at one of his two watches. He had one on each wrist. They were great chunky things with stubby hands. The watches were large as well.

"Look at the time," said Kong. "Any minute now and the bell will be going . . ."

From away in the distance came a clanging sound. Triv looked at his own watch. One o'clock. The lunch break had ended and the St Ethelred's bell was ringing to say so.

". . . going . . ."

It seemed to Triv that Kong's voice had changed. It was distant, somehow.

". . . going," droned Kong, ". . . going . . . GOING!"

And then he was – gone; springing off as fast as he could towards the St Ethelred's buildings in the distance.

Triv watched in amazement. So did the duck, as Kong ran through its pond instead of round it.

"Five!" cried Triv. "The fifth bell!"

The duck gave him a quizzical look, but then it hadn't been to the *Olde Tyme Music Hall* and seen The Great Wallendo hold five fingers in front of Kong's baffled face while he muttered something that nobody could hear.

Five. Five bells. Morning registration. Morning break start. Morning break end. Lunch break start. Lunch break end. Five ringings of the school bell.

Of course! It all made sense now.

"That's why they didn't come back from lunch!" Triv told the duck.

With renewed energy he started back. Far ahead of him he saw that Kong, still travelling at speed, had reached the boundary fence. It took Triv fifteen minutes to get to the same spot but, when he did, this time he didn't need any help in climbing over.

He simply stepped through the Kong-shaped hole and headed for school.

\* \* \*

A welcoming party was waiting for him as he staggered up to the school gates. Except that it wasn't terribly welcoming, the party concerned being Madeleine.

"At last!" she said, dabbing at her eyes with a big cotton handkerchief. "Oh, I've been so worried about you!"

Triv was exhausted. He leant against the wall. "Kong . . ." he gasped.

"He came back ages ago!" cried Madeleine. "Ages!"

"W- . . ." started Triv, then ran out of breath.

71

"Where? Here, of course."

"Wall- . . ."

"Wall?" Madeleine looked confused for a moment, then the dawn of understanding lit up her eyes. "You want to lean against a wall, poppet? I understand, you must be absolutely puffed out." She rushed to his side and led him over to the end wall of the bike sheds.

"Wallend- . . ."

"Wall end?" Madeleine Mooney was confused again. "This is the end wall."

"Hyp- . . ."

"Hip? What about your hip? It hurts, is that what you're trying to say? I'm not surprised darling, what with all that running those leggy-peggies have been doing."

"Hypnotist!" gasped Triv, finally getting enough breath into his lungs to say a complete word. "Wallendo!" Gasp. "Great!" Gasp. "The!" The effort left him leaning against the wall. Gasping.

From the other side came the rattle of a bicycle chain. Then the angry pulling of the chain's bicycle from its place between two others. Finally the chain's bicycle's owner, wheeling the machine as though it had just done something to offend her.

Susan Frost was livid.

"James is back, Susan," said Madeleine, pointing towards the wheezing Triv.

As Susan Frost glanced in his direction, Triv thought he might be in line for another sympathetic kiss. His hopes were dashed. She simply said "So I see", and then, with her nose inclined ever-so-slightly in the air, glanced away again.

"I am taking industrial action!" she declared to the world at large. "That man King has gone too far!"

Triv gave her a steely look. Two kisses in one day might have been a lot to expect, but some show of feeling was not. If Kong had gone too far with anyone, it was him. Round and round the duckpond for a start.

"*This*," Susan proclaimed, dipping into her shoulder bag, "is an important document." She waved a sheet of music manuscript in the air. "This is my *own* composition. For next term's Music Festival. For the sake of St Ethelred's I have spent *hours* on this. Now look at the state it's in!"

What about the state I'm in? thought Triv. So, her sheet of paper had stains all over it. She could produce another one. Unclapping a clapped-out James Trevellyan was a different matter or couldn't the stupid girl see that?

"It's tea, isn't it?" said Madeleine Mooney, wrinkling her nose.

"I don't care *what* it is!" screamed Susan Frost. "It could be creosote for all I care! All I know is that I was walking along when that awful man ran into me and slopped this . . ." the manuscript shook in anger ". . . whatever it is all over it."

"Tea," said Madeleine Mooney solemnly. "Definitely tea." Her nose gave another wrinkle. "Quick Brew, I'd say . . . and . . ." sniff, wrinkle, sniff, "probably tea-bags."

"All over it!" Susan Frost wailed again. "Almost a whole cupful."

"Sounds like you've been mugged," said Triv, laughing, "Get it? Mug, tea."

Susan gave him the sort of look that would have turned milk to yoghurt. "He didn't even stop to apologize, James! He simply guffawed and carried on."

"A hit and fun driver, eh?"

"This is not a laughing matter!"

Triv laughed. Not very well, because it hurt. But enough to show Susan Frost that if his blistered feet, rubberized legs and scorched lungs hadn't deserved any sympathy from her, then a few tea stains on a sheet of music weren't going to get any from him.

"James!! I am not amused!"

"Belt up," said Triv. Susan Frost, the divine Susan, with whom he'd dreamed of sharing an apple bite by bite until their lips met at the core, was starting to give him the pip.

"I beg your pardon!"

"Belt up," repeated Triv.

"Honeybun, really!" cried Madeleine, shocked. "Say you didn't mean it."

"I did mean it," said Triv. "And I'm not your honeybun, so you can belt up too! Now . . ."

He waded in while the stunned silence still gave him the chance.

"Kong has been hypnotized. He's in a trance. That's why he didn't stop when he bumped into you, Susan. He's obeying The Great Wallendo's orders – whatever they are."

"Magnificent," purred Madeleine.

She found the new, commanding, Triv even more attractive than the old gentle one. It could only be a matter of time before he whacked her over the head and dragged her off to his cave.

"The school bell triggered things off," Triv said.

74

"The fifth ring of the day. That's why none of them came back from lunch."

Susan Frost was slowly regaining her composure. Madeleine Mooney wasn't the only one who had been affected by being told to belt up. The difference, however, was that whereas Madeleine had become moonier, Susan had become frostier.

"In that case," she said, her voice like burnt toast being scraped, "why did Mr Winkler disappear after school last Wednesday? He didn't turn up at all on Thursday if you remember. Mastermind," she added triumphantly.

"Susan's right, gumdrop," said Madeleine. "He's part-time. He's not here Tuesdays and Fridays. Or Wednesday morning."

"Well, brains?" Susan was gloating.

Inspiration struck. "The Tuesday Matinee!" shouted Triv.

"What?"

"The fifth bell. If he went to the Tuesday matinee and didn't come into school until just before lunchtime on Wednesday then when would he have heard the fifth bell?"

"I don't know . . ."

"Two lunch bells, two afternoon break bells . . . and the going home bell would have been his fifth!"

"Wonderful," sighed Madeleine Mooney. "Isn't he just wonderful, Susan? I believe him, don't you?"

Susan Frost bit her lip. Admitting she was wrong after being told to belt up was not going to come easily.

"I do," Madeleine Mooney burbled on. "And I

bet if we went up to Kong's study right now we'd find a note on his door!"

* * *

They did. And there wasn't.

As the three of them stood outside, Triv tried not to show his concern. But concerned he was.

"Maybe . . . maybe it's on his desk," he said.

"Oh yes?" said Susan Frost. Feeling a victory coming on she rattled the door open and marched in, with Madeleine close behind. Triv came in third, as good a position as he'd ever managed.

"Pooh!" cried Madeleine. "What's that pong?"

Six eyes and three noses swung unerringly towards the source of the pong. Perched on the windowsill, wisps of steam still curling gently from them, sat Kong's running shoes.

"No sign of any note," said Susan coolly.

Triv headed round the side of Kong's desk and examined it closely. Something was different.

He tried to think about what he'd seen on his last visit. Piles of lines, yes. Pens, yes. Piles of lines, folders, an in-tray, an out-tray, piles and piles of lines. Yes, yes, yes, yes, yes and yes. Ingo English crouching beneath Kong's desk hoping he wouldn't be seen but realizing that he had been? No.

"Ah . . ." said Ingo.

"Ingo!" exclaimed Susan. "What on earth are you doing there?"

"Er . . . looking, weren't I?"

"What for?" asked Triv."

"For . . . for your benefit, Triv old mate."

Triv had to give Ingo credit for quick thinking. Pockets bulging with confiscated chewing gum

76

and joke books, and he could still lie his way out of a corner without batting an eyelid.

"Saw old Kong come back didn't I?" said Ingo. "Then I saw him go out again. And I thought, poor old Triv, he's probably got him up here writing lines again."

"And you came to assist your friend," said Susan Frost. "Even if he deserved everything he got," she snapped.

"Got it in one, Susie," Ingo agreed happily. "A friend in need is a friend . . ."

"Indeed, Ingo," said Susan. "And did you," she added, "find a note by any chance?"

"Yes," said Madeleine, "did you find a note?"

Ingo shook his head. "Nope. Didn't touch a thing. Well . . . apart from them." He pointed at Kong's running shoes, still humming to themselves on the windowsill. "Put 'em on the chair, hadn't he? What a stink!"

Triv's stomach did a somersault. He went over to the windowsill and, holding his nose, picked up the shoes.

"Look!" exclaimed Madeleine.

They looked. An exclamation mark had been drawn on the bottom of the left shoe and a question mark on the sole of the right.

"What does it mean?"

"It means what we've always reckoned," said Ingo. "Kong ain't got no sole!"

"Idiot," said Susan Frost. She looked sheepishly at Triv. "It's a message, isn't it?"

"Of course it is!" shrieked Madeleine Mooney. "It means . . . what does it mean, lollipop?"

Triv looked at his watch. Yes, he calculated, he

could afford to keep them in suspense for five minutes or so.

"Work it out for yourselves," he said with the air of a master detective who knew whodunnit. "I won't be long."

He hurried down to the changing room and climbed back into his St Ethelred's uniform. A quick ferret through the pockets of his blazer unearthed what he needed.

He arrived back in Kong's study to find Susan Frost, Madeleine Mooney and Ingo English still looking as baffled as when he'd left.

"Well?" he asked. "What's the message?"

"No idea," said Susan reluctantly. "You win."

Triv hoped he was looking coldly superior as he pointed first at the shoe with an exclamation mark scrawled on its sole, then at the one with the question mark.

"Left! Right?"

\* \* \*

"So what do you suggest we do now?" asked Susan Frost.

"We go after him," said Triv.

"Great!" yelled Ingo. "Like in the films. Follow him to the villain's hideout!"

"He's been gone for ages," pointed out Susan. "What do we do, commandeer a taxi?"

"That's it!" Ingo was racing for the door. "I'll do the talking. I know the lingo, see. *Follow that car*," he snarled dramatically.

"He isn't driving a car," said Susan Frost. "Idiot."

"The solution is quite simple," said Triv coolly. He straightened his tie, then looked at his watch. The time was right. With a flick of his wrist, Triv nonchalantly whipped the vital information from his jacket pocket.

He could tell they were impressed by the way they stared at it.

"But dumbly-bumbly," began Madeleine Mooney, "that's a . . ."

"Bus timetable," confirmed Triv. "A number 17 is what we want. There'll be one along any minute now."

\* \* \*

Watling couldn't make it out at all.

Munching his sandwiches in the library – the *Encyclopaedia Britannica* flattened them out nicely, he'd discovered – he'd watched the goings-on in the playground with mounting confusion.

First of all he'd seen Kong come galloping back through the school gates.

Then, a few minutes later, he'd seen him go galloping out again, this time bare-footed and with a mug in his hand.

Then that neat bird Madeleine Mooney had come out to hang around waiting for brain-box Trevellyan.

No sooner had brain-box Trevellyan come back than that snooty Susan Frost had come out of the bike-sheds with her bike.

Then she'd put it back again and all three of them had buzzed off somewhere.

Now they were back again, this time with Ingo in tow.

Something's missing, thought Watling, as he watched them run out of the school gates and leap on to a number 17 bus.

It took him a couple of minutes to realize what it was that was missing.

It was him. They'd gone off without him, rotten lot.

Right!

Moments later he too was heading out of St Ethelred's and following the route of the number 17. He looked a touch guilty as he pedalled furiously along the road, but never mind. Susan Frost wasn't using her bike and it was quicker than walking.

# 10
# Triv in pursuit

"I suppose you think you're very clever," said Susan.

Triv shrugged. They were sitting on the top deck, Susan and Madeleine sharing the back seat, with Triv just in front of them. Ingo was up at the front, waving his arms about and making brrmm-ing noises.

"He is," said Madeleine Mooney. "Nobody else but my petal would have known a number 17 gets its own little bit of road to use all the way."

Triv smiled. From outside St Ethelred's, as he could have told them, the bus lane turns left into Market Way, right into Western Avenue, left once again into High Street and then, via two roundabouts and a pelican crossing, into Ripple Road. Tootling along it, a number 17 bus could outstrip James Bond in his Aston Martin.

"There he is!" shouted Ingo.

They looked out of the window. Down below, still in his tracksuit and still clutching the blue-and-white hooped mug he'd been carrying when he collided with Susan Frost, Kong was striding purposefully along the pavement.

"It doesn't look like he's in a trance to me," Susan said.

"Oh no?" said Triv.

"Yes it does," said Susan.

Kong, finding a parked car in his way, had opened a rear door, stepped through, and popped out of the other side.

"Shouldn't we get off and stop him?" asked Madeleine.

"Before he does any damage," said Susan, as, below them, Kong marched through a flower-bed.

"Yeah, come on!" shouted Ingo, bounding to the head of the stairway. "We should grab him, and torture him 'til he spills the beans."

Triv shook his head slowly. "Not yet."

"When then?" said Ingo.

"When the bus stops."

Susan Frost was looking at him with a new respect. "And where does it stop?" she asked.

"I know," squealed Madeleine Mooney. "I know, I know." She was looking ahead, her eyes aglow. "I know! It's the supermarket!"

She was right. The grey-brick building loomed larger and larger as the bus trundled towards it. Flags fluttered along the length of its frontage, as though they were the Royal Family arriving to do their weekly shopping.

BBB's – the Supermarket for Bargain Buys in Bulk – awaited them.

The bus dropped them at the front door.

* * *

As Kong sprinted their way, Triv deployed his troops.

"Cover all the entrances," he commanded.

Ingo English made a rude noise. "There's only one. Over there." He pointed to a self-opening glass door.

"Just testing," said Triv. He looked back. Kong

82

was getting closer, now vaulting over a line of wire trolleys like a steeplechaser dealing with the water jump.

"Why don't we go inside, lemon-drop?" said Madeleine Mooney. "Then we can see where he goes."

"Sounds sensible to me Madeleine," said Susan. "What do you think, Napoleon?"

Triv ignored the jibe. "Just what I was going to suggest," he said. "Right. Let's go."

They dived through the glass doors and across to where boxes of cornflakes, wheatflakes, branflakes, coco-flakes, honeyflakes and nutty-flakes were piled on shelving which stretched away as far as the eye could see. A long-running cereal, in other words.

It was the ideal spot, with a perfect view of the entrance. Triv ushered the others to his side and waited.

And waited.

And waited.

"Where is he?" Triv muttered. "He should be here by now."

"Perhaps he's changed his mind," said Susan.

"He can't change his mind," retorted Triv. "He isn't in charge of it. He's doing whatever The Great Wallendo told him to do."

Ingo clicked his fingers, as though the answer to all known problems had just come to him.

"Maybe he's not doing what we think he thinks he's doing. Maybe he's doing something else and making us come in here is a whatsit . . . red mackerel."

"Herring," said Madeleine, one eye drifting towards the fresh fish counter.

"A red herring!" exclaimed Triv. "Of course! The Great Wallendo wouldn't have wanted to arouse suspicion by having Kong march through the store. He'd have got him to go . . ."

"Round the back way!" Ingo was on his feet in a trice, pulling Susan Frost behind him. "Let's go, baby!"

Before Triv could argue, the pair of them were outside the shop and racing along behind a large delivery van as it made its way to the rear entrance. He went to follow them, but Madeleine laid a hand on his arm.

"We could take a short-cut," she said, pointing. "That way."

Triv looked. Beyond an aisle of freezers stood a door marked "Private".

"Where does it go?"

Madeleine shrugged. "Not sure," she said, but a strange glow had come into her eyes.

This was no time to be cautious. Triv grabbed hold of an empty shopping trolley to make it look as if he were just a normal customer and started to push his way over to the door.

Reaching it, Triv glanced right and left. Nobody was looking his way. Within moments he had pushed his trolley through the door and into the room beyond.

"Oooohh!" sighed Madeleine Mooney, following behind him. She looked as if she'd arrived in heaven.

The room was not so much a room as a cavern. A cavern piled from floor to ceiling with things to eat.

"This way," urged Triv.

"In a minute."

As Triv pushed the trolley deeper into the cavern, towards another door at the far end, from behind him came the sound of strong teeth beginning to chomp their way through a packet of gingernut biscuits.

"Come on!" he called.

"Phhssst," came the reply.

The only problem with gingernut biscuits, Madeleine had found, was that they made you terribly thirsty. So finding a cherryade tower right next to the gingernut mountain was a double bonus. Phhssst, went another can of cherryade.

"Come on!" said Triv again.

Crunch and hiss, crunch and hiss. Madeleine was into her stride. "Id a binid," she called.

The door at the far end had a small glass panel set into it. As Triv reached it, he peered through. He blinked and peered again but the sight remained unchanged. He was looking at a corridor that he'd seen before. A corridor that he walked every weekday. A St Ethelred's corridor.

It was complete in every way. The colour scheme, of grey and olive green, was right. The doors, especially the one marked "Staff Room", were right. Everything was right. Even down to the two pupils in St Ethelred's uniforms who were knocking on the door.

The only thing that wasn't right was that Susan Frost and Ingo English were knocking on the door, not with their hands, but with their heads. This, in turn, was due to the fact that a large man with a white coat and a black beard had them gripped by the scruff of the neck.

As Triv watched, the door swung open and a rosy red face popped out.

"Hello, ducks," it said, "come and join the party."

Triv recognized the face immediately, even though the last time he'd seen it was when it had been stuck behind a grille. Of course! Who better to be sending out free tickets than the Globe Theatre's Box Office lady?

And who better to be in cahoots with the bearded man now shoving Susan Frost and Ingo English into the room? A man known, outside the world of bulk bargain buying, by another name.

"In there you two," growled The Great Wallendo.

*　*　*

To a girl like Susan Frost, it looked like a gold charm that was twinkling before her eyes.

To a boy like Ingo English it looked more like the badge on a policeman's helmet: shiny and impossible to take your eyes off, even though you wanted to run a mile.

To Mr Stitson, Miss Derbyshire, Mr McDougall, Mr Winkler and Mademoiselle Balmain, seated unmoving and glassy-eyed around the walls of the room, it was something they'd seen before but couldn't remember where.

To the track-suited Kong it was familiar too — although for some reason he thought it should be shaped like a rubber bone.

But to The Great Wallendo, hypnotist extraordinaire, the gold medallion meant most of all. It meant power.

He started it swinging, fixing Susan Frost and Ingo English with his piercing eyes.

"You are both feeling very tired," he droned.

Leaving Madeleine to the gingernuts and cherry-ade, Triv had tiptoed along the corridor. Through the door at the end he could hear the sound of The Great Wallendo's voice.

"You are my servants," he heard him say. "You will not move a muscle . . ."

Triv edged closer, crouching down so that his ear was at the keyhole.

". . . Until I say the key word . . ."

This is it! thought Triv. He screwed his eyes tight, his whole mind concentrating on the softly persuasive voice on the other side of the door. All hypnotists had a way of getting their victims out of a trance. Some snapped their fingers, but clearly The Great Wallendo used the key word technique.

". . . the key word which will make you obey my every command . . ."

Triv listened as he'd never listened before.

". . . the key word, which is . . ."

"Boo!"

Triv couldn't have jumped any higher if he'd suddenly discovered he was standing in a tub of maggots without any socks on.

"Aaagh!" he yelled.

"Tee-hee-hee," Madeleine giggled. "It's only little me. What's going on?"

Triv thought quickly. What would he do if he was inside a room and heard a yell of "aaagh!" coming from outside? He would investigate, that's what.

For once, his gentlemanly instincts deserted him. Without giving Madeleine a second glance he dashed back down the corridor and into the storeroom.

Behind him he heard a muffled cry, like a mouth with gingernut biscuits in it being covered by a hand with a medallion in it; then the click of a door being closed; then silence.

* * *

"You are feeling very tired."

The Great Wallendo was starting to feel pretty tired himself. In front of him, her face stern and defiant, sat Madeleine.

"You know where you can stick your medallion, don't you?" She said it with spirit, but her eyes told the sad story. She was beginning to droop.

"Very tired," insisted The Great Wallendo.

He was winning, at last. This one had put up a real struggle. Slowly, like a parachutist coming in to land, Madeleine's eyelids descended.

But Madeleine had a stout heart inside her skinny frame. For one last, belligerent moment her eyes sprung open.

"You wait," she hollered. "My scrummy-bundle knows all about you! He's . . . here . . . some . . . where . . ."

* * *

Her scrummy-bundle, after dashing back along the corridor to the sanctuary of the cavernous storeroom, was feeling grim. A few seconds more and he'd have found out about The Great Wallendo's key word. Then he could have dashed in, yelled it at the top of his voice and . . . well, he wasn't quite sure what would have happened but it would have been worth a try.

But without it, he was stuck. Dashing in and working his way through the *Oxford Dictionary* would take too long – especially if Wallendo's key word was something like "xylophone" or "zip-a-dee-doo-dah."

What he needed was a second chance to listen in to the hypnotist at work . . .

Of course! In the panic he'd overlooked one slight detail. Madeleine Mooney.

The Great Wallendo was probably trying to hypnotize her at that very moment. He started to edge his way back along the corridor, then changed his mind.

There was no point in going to look for The Great Wallendo.

For one thing, the hypnotist was a very busy man and wouldn't take kindly to being disturbed.

And, for another, because at that moment The Great Wallendo was coming along the corridor looking for him.

\* \* \*

Triv backed away as the storeroom door creaked open. As a beard entered, he backed even further away.

And as the remainder of The Great Wallendo appeared he backed into the shopping trolley he'd pushed into the storeroom a little earlier. The beard whirled round in the direction of the noise.

"Oy, you! Come here!"

The voice wasn't hypnotic but it had an immediate effect on Triv. He ran.

"Come here, I said!"

Dodging between a stack of baked beans and a pillar of marmalade, Triv's intention was straightforward. It was to run straight forward, until he reached the door which led out into the supermarket itself.

Behind him, The Great Wallendo was breathing hard. Triv was nearly there. Safety loomed.

Unfortunately, so did somebody else.

"Get him Else," yelled The Great Wallendo.

"Slow down, ducks."

In through the door had stepped the red-faced ticket woman.

Triv skidded to a halt. He looked around, but it was no use. He'd been outflanked. On both sides towered the gingernut biscuits and cherryade cans, no lower even after Madeleine's attention.

In front of him, hands on hips, stood Ticket-Woman. And behind . . . he knew who was behind him.

A man, as James Bond might have said if he'd been in the same position, of influence.

\* \* \*

"You are feeling very tired."

So this was what it was like to be hypnotized, thought Triv. He was struggling to keep his eyes open.

"Awkward little herbert, ain't he, Charlie?"

"He is, Else, he is."

"Charlie?" mumbled Triv. His drowsy brain struggled with this unexpected piece of information. The Great Charlie? No, that wasn't right. "What happened to The Great Wallendo?"

"Nothing," growled the bearded wonder. "Charlie Tomkins and The Great Wallendo are one and the same."

"Charlie! Don't say nuffink."

90

"Don't worry Else. He won't remember none of it when I'm done with him." He spun the medallion a little faster. "I only do Great Wallendoing part-time, see? During the day I'm Charlie Tomkins . . ."

"*Manager* of BBB's," said red-face proudly. "And I'm Elsie Tomkins . . ."

"Checkout Operative and Part-time Box Officer for the Globe Theatre," chipped in the hypnotist. "So now you know it all."

Triv shook his head. It was starting to feel as if it was stuffed with feathers.

"Why . . . why . . ." he murmured. "Kong and . . . the others . . . why? What for?"

"I need them," said The Great Wallendo, "Teachers have a special talent, you see."

"Oh yes," echoed Else, "a special talent."

Triv's brain stirred again. It always had responded well to riddles.

Mental images popped up like ducks on a rifle range. Mr Stitson, mug in hand, comparing Triv's ashtray to a flying saucer; Miss Derbyshire criticizing 'View from a Flagpole' before returning to her electric fire and steaming cup; Mr McDougall, Mr Winkler and Mademoiselle Balmain, sitting together in the refreshment lounge of the Dover-Calais ferry on their one-day educational outing to France; and Kong . . . Kong hurdling his way through the traffic that very day, holding on grimly to his blue-and-white mug.

"Tea!" exclaimed Triv. "They're always drinking tea!"

"Correct," said Charlie Tomkins/The Great Wallendo.

"Proper connersewers they are," enthused red-face, still leaning against the exit door.

"Were I a joking man," said Tomkins, "I would say that's how the 'tea' got into 'teacher'. But I am not a joking man. And tea is a serious business. Ain't that right, Else?"

"It is, Charlie, it is."

The beard looked hard at Triv. "Have you got any idea how many cups of tea the British drink every day?"

"Thirty-three million, four hundred thousand," said Triv instantly. Considering that the hypnotist wanted to put him to sleep, he couldn't have been doing more to keep him awake if he'd been trying.

"Er . . . that's right."

"Smart Alec as well, eh?" said Else.

"So a man, call him Charlie Tomkins say," said Charlie Tomkins/The Great Wallendo "who can make his own teabags out of a special formula of two parts tea-leaves, two parts cheap flour and one part free sawdust from the DIY shop round the corner, and who can get a bunch of teachers to test it for him until he gets the flavour right, that man stands to make pots of money . . ."

"Out of pots of tea," cackled Else.

"None of which you are going to remember, young man."

The medallion was spinning, faster and faster. So was Triv's head now.

"You will forget everything you have been told," droned Charlie Tomkins in his Great Wallendo voice, "and you are going to stay here until I say the key word . . ."

"The key word," echoed Triv.

"Which is . . ."

"Which is?"

". . . Pomegranate. Got that?"

"Pomegranate," murmured Triv. "Pomegranate."

He felt himself going, drifting away like a sailing boat in a gentle breeze. So this was what it was like to be hypnotized. You felt drowsier and drowsier, sleepier and sleepier, and then . . .

And then you heard a terrific racket as though the roof was falling in, followed by screams and shouts and the sound of people being hit on the head by heavy objects? Surely not.

But that *is* what's happening, signalled Triv's brain to his eyes. They opened, to check for themselves.

And never, ever, had those eyes been as glad to see what they did. Nor, for that matter, his ears as glad to hear the words of one whose presence normally spelt catastrophe with a capital K.

"What you doing there, Trevellyan?" said Watling.

\* \* \*

After leaving St Ethelred's, Watling had followed the route of the number 17 bus as quickly as he was able. As far as physical dimensions were concerned, however, he'd found that his own had little in common with those of Susan Frost. Pedalling a bike with his toes scraping the ground and his knees six inches above the handlebars had made for slow progress.

It had almost meant disaster too. Not far from BBB's – the supermarket for Bargain Bulk Buying – his knees had got in the way once too

93

often and he'd careered into the path of a number 17 bus coming down the road. But, for once, Lady Fortune had smiled on him.

Not only had the driver screeched to a halt in time. The man had also opened his little window and screamed something about not knowing what the roads were coming to what with dozy bike riders and hurdling joggers all over the show. Then he'd started to bang his head against his steering wheel.

In an inspired moment Watling had connected the bus with the one he'd seen Ingo and Co get on outside St Ethelred's, and the jogger with Kong. They had to be near. Besides which, he fancied a drink after all that pedalling and there he was, outside a supermarket.

BBB's sold everything. Everything apart, or so it seemed, from what he really fancied: a can of cherryade. All gone.

Vaguely he remembered this happening to him once before and a nice lady going through a door somewhere to find some more. A door just like the one he could see. It was marked "Private" but there hadn't seemed to be any nice ladies around this time so he'd gone over to it. And pushed. It had been a bit stiff, so he'd pushed again. A lot harder.

And that was how Elsie Tomkins, leaning against the other side of this door, had found herself suddenly shooting forwards. Unable to stop, she'd hurtled straight past husband Charlie and towards the tower of cherryade cans that Madeleine had dipped into earlier.

Dipped into, rather naughtily, by taking cans from the middle of the tower rather than the top, so that the whole structure needed only the slight-est touch to make it come crashing down.

The roof-falling-in sounds, Triv could now see, had been due not to the roof falling in but the cherryade can tower collapsing. Mostly on top of Charlie 'The Great Wallendo' Tomkins and his wife Else, which also accounted for the sounds of heavy objects landing on heads.

"Hang on to them, Watters!" shouted Triv. Groaning gently, the pair were stirring.

Watling, happy that for once a scene of devas-tation hadn't led to him being moaned at, did as he was told. With a cheery smile and a lot of enthusiasm, he wrapped an arm around each of the groaner's necks and held them tight.

Triv, in the meantime, had dropped to his knees and was ferreting amongst the cans.

"Ah-ah!" he said in triumph.

He stood up again, in his hands the gold med-allion that The Great Wallendo had dropped when the cherryade tower had fallen on him.

He looked at the hypnotist, then down at the medallion. He looked at Else, the hypnotist's wife, then back at the medallion again. It was an out-side chance, Triv thought, but it might work.

Suspending the medallion in front of Watling's prisoners he gently started it swinging.

"You are feeling very tired," he said, "very, very tired indeed."

Charlie Tomkins flicked his eyes open. On the other side, Else did the same.

"You are feeling whacked out. Ready for bed," intoned Triv.

Amazingly, there in front of him, Charlie Tomkins – The Great Wallendo himself – started to go glassy-eyed. So too, in a touching display of togetherness, did his wife.

It was working!

"I am going to give you a command and you will obey me without question. Do you hear me?"

"I hear you."

"I hear you."

"I hear you."

Triv looked around. The storeroom was large, but he hadn't noticed an echo before.

"When I snap my fingers you will walk slowly out of here, down the corridor, and through the door at the end. Do you understand?"

"I do."

"I do."

"I do," echoed the echo.

This is it, thought Triv. The acid test. 'OK Watters," he said, "let them go."

Charlie and Else, released from Watling's heavy grip, swayed slightly. Triv snapped his fingers.

The effect was instantaneous.

"I must obey," said the hypnotist in a leaden voice. And with that he walked slowly across the storeroom and out into the corridor.

"I must obey," said Elsie Tomkins and promptly followed in her husband's footsteps.

Triv was jubilant. He'd done it!

"Just call me The Great Trevello!" he cried. "What do you think of that, Watters?"

"I must obey," said Watling the echo as he headed for the door.

# 11

# A position of influence

Triv had a problem.

Well, thirteen problems to be absolutely accur-
ate, and all of them gathered silently together in
the replica St Ethelred's staff room.

The school group sounded like the tail end of an
alternative *Twelve Days of Christmas*: four silent
pupils, three dumb men teachers, two lady
learneds and a Kong sitting on a settee.

Add a hypnotized hypnotist and a hypnotized
hypnotist's wife huddled together in a corner, and
you had twelve of Triv's thirteen problems.

The thirteenth problem was rather different. It
wasn't a hypnotized person. It was the little
matter of Triv not being able to remember The
Great Wallendo's key word.

Unless he could remember it, he was stuck.
They all were. What had The Great Wallendo said
to him out there in the storeroom?

Triv's memory of what had happened was pretty
misty. He could remember the medallion waving
about in front of his eyes. And he could remember
feeling very tired.

Yes, and he could remember a voice, a soothing
voice, telling him to forget all about something
and to stay somewhere until he heard the special
word. What he couldn't remember was what that

97

special word was. He tried a few possibilities at random.

'Rumplestiltskin!"

Nothing. Nobody moved. Nobody even murmured.

"Fried bananas!"

The twelve stayed silent.

Triv still had the medallion in his hand. As he looked at it, something stirred in the back of his mind.

Medallion.

Medal? No.

Olympic Games? No.

Marathon running? No.

Tossing the caber? No, wrong games. Mentioning that might be enough to get Mr McDougall going, but it would leave the rest cold.

"Hop, step and jump!" he tried without much hope. No. He was on the right track though, he was sure of that.

Olympic Games.

Opening ceremony? No.

Flags? No.

Union Jack? No.

Countries? England? France? Outer Mongolia? Australia . . .

He got that stirring sensation again. Something about Australia? Was it that?

"Kangaroo!" Hopeless. Not a flicker.

Something about England? No.

England *and* Australia? Yes, yes.

Didgeridoo? No.

Rolf Harris? No.

What did they call an Australian – Aussie! Was that it? No.

The other way round then. What do Australians call the English?

"Chinless wonders!" he yelled. No, that wasn't it.

Pommie! That was it.

The stir in his mind stirred like crazy. Triv looked at the gold medallion again, hoping for one final blast of inspiration.

Pommie athlete? No.

Pommie javelin thrower? No.

Pommie runner? No.

Pommie runner winning a gold medal? No.

Pommie runner pipped at the post? No.

Pommie pipped? No. Pipped Pommie? No. Pommie with a load of pips . . . yes!! That was it! Pomegranate!!!!!!

\* \* \*

Triv paced backwards and forwards, deep in thought. Finally he stopped. Yes, that was it. That's what he would do.

So long as the key word did its stuff, that was. Theory was all well and good, but it was practice that mattered. He needed someone to practise on. Somebody without much in the way of mental resistance.

"Watling," he said softly. "Listen to me. The word 'pomegranate' means something special to you."

"No it don't," said Watling.

"It does. When I say that word you will leave here and return from whence you came . . . do you understand me?"

"No," said Watling.

"Leave," said Triv. "Go."

"On me bike, you mean? Right."

Moving close, Triv whispered "pomegranate".

"Pomegranate."

Watling blinked. He looked around as though he didn't know where he was or what on earth was going on.

It had worked. Watling was acting normally.

Watling turned and headed for the door. He stopped, one hand on the door knob, as though trying to remember what he'd been told to do.

And then he was gone, his heavy footsteps plonking along the corridor outside.

\* \* \*

Triv turned his attention to Charlie Tomkins and wife.

"Does the word 'pomegranate' mean anything to either of you?" he said.

"Fresh fruit counter," said Elsie Tomkins at once, "seventy-three pence a pound."

Charlie Tomkins seemed to be thinking a bit harder. "It is my key word," he droned. "The key word I use to unlock my victims from their hypnotic trances."

His wife nodded. "And that. It is the key that unlocks what he said."

Triv looked from one to the other. "It is my key word too. When I say it you will immediately forget all that's happened in the past week." He added, "and be coffee-drinkers from now on. Pomegranate."

Triv stood back as the pair linked hands and walked to the door.

"Come on, Else,' said Charlie Tomkins. "The VAT forms are waiting."

"Oh, Charlie. You and your managing. Let's have a nice cuppa coffee first . . ."

* * *

The five teachers were next.

"You will all forget what has happened to you this week," said Triv softly. He paused, with "pomegranate" on his lips.

Could he? Should he? Why not?

"And you, Miss Derbyshire, will decide that 'View From A Flagpole' by James Trevellyan, 3B, is absolutely brilliant and worth the art prize at least . . ."

"I will," agreed Miss Derbyshire, "I will find it hot stuff."

"Mr Stitson," Triv said, "you will think my ash tray is a superbly original design, and well worth the metalwork prize. Mr McDougall, you will think I'm a bright laddie and let me interrupt you at any time with my interesting facts. You, Mademoiselle Balmain, will suddenly get it into your head that my talent for French would be helped by an invitation to spend a week or two in Paris during the summer holidays. And you, Mr Winkler . . . you will turf me out of the music room whenever Susan Frost is practising. Do you all understand?'

"Ye-es," they said together.

"Then all I've got to say is . . . pomegranate!"

* * *

Telling old Mr Winkler to keep him away from Susan Frost had been a carefully considered move.

Girls, Triv had decided, were trouble. He'd writ-

101

ten lines by the thousand, spent a small fortune on beefburgers and theatre tickets, been in a fountain and round and round a lake because of girls and that was quite enough, thank you very much.

He was going to retire from girls and go back to his first love, *The Guinness Book of Records*.

"Susan and Madeleine," he said quietly, "When I say the key word, you will forget everything that has happened."

"What, me and all?" It was Ingo English, leaning against the wall and looking like a dead fish.

Ingo. Triv had almost forgotten about him. The two girls had caused him trouble, but Ingo hadn't helped either.

A smile spread across Triv's face. Could he? Should he? Why not?

"Ingo . . ." he said smoothly, "you will decide that Susan isn't the object of your desires any more. You will realize that Madeleine is much more your type."

Triv turned to Madeleine. "And you, Madeleine, will find that James Trevellyan – in spite of his fantastic charm – isn't quite scrummy enough. In fact you'll decide that Ingo English is the scrummiest, bundliest boy you've ever seen."

Finally, he turned to gaze into what he would once have described as liquid pools of azure, but which were in fact simply Susan Frost's blue eyes. He could see, now, that she wasn't really his type. Too big for her boots. No, she was much more suited to someone else. Someone with even bigger boots.

"And Susan," said Triv, "you will have an uncontrollable urge to go out with a person who's got uncontrollable size nine feet."